CW00482133

Dark Nephilim

Always Dark Angel Series
Book Two
Edition 1 2017
Copyright © 2017 JN Moon
GrippingReadsLtd Production Ltd

Acknowledgements

I WOULD LIKE TO THANK my friends who have stuck by me and supported me during the highs and lows of writing this. And the family I live with who have barely seen me for months as I disappear into the writing cave when I'm not out in the world for the day job. I hope one day soon to have a holiday...

Licence Notes.

This eBook is licensed for your personal enjoyment only. This eBook may not be re-sold or given away to other people. If you would like to share this book with another person, please purchase an additional copy for each recipient.

Publisher's Note.

This is a work of fiction. Names and characters are either fictitious or the product of the author's imagination. Any resemblance to actual persons, living or dead, business establishments, events or locales is entirely coincidental.

Make Contact

To receive my monthly newsletter, get awesome free stuff or be an ARC Reader just click here... **alwaysdarkangel.com**

Facebook Group: ***Moon Council of the Supernatural***[1] : join to see cover reveals, behind the scenes and discuss all things supernatural.

---

1. *https://www.facebook.com/groups/247165435816384/*

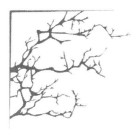

Prologue

THEY CROUCHED ON TOP of the Georgian buildings, their massive wings beating slowly. Looking down as the mortals passed unawares, these magnificent and terrifying creatures were watching, waiting. Waiting for blood; their once milky skin, now shining obsidian, crimson tinged. Red from the blood they stole, blood that they were not designed to take. Crimson that glistened under the slight moonlight in that picturesque city. Like something from a macabre Gothic tale, hair flowing in the wind and their hands gripping the ledges, their movements animalistic. But then they'd never been human.

Watching them from my hiding place, they jumped down one by one and blended effortlessly into society. Their wings remained hidden from mortal eyes by some trick, but I didn't know how. I stayed hidden otherwise they'd take my blood for sure. They'd smell it and they would bleed me dry. But not all my kin were so fortunate to escape their grasp.

These creatures were muscular, unnaturally tall with the confidence of a hundred kings. Each of them were forbidden by nature and answerable to no-one. They searched for my kind who they'd spent thousands of years killing remorselessly as they viewed us as an abomination, a plague upon the land. And now they sought us to devour our blood, our souls. It had driven them into a frenzy, the taste of blood, that swoon, hungry and savage.

These creatures changed the design of their nature from killing my kin, to feeding off of us. We, the hunters, became the hunted, and we had to hide and out-manoeuvre these dark nephilim that were once divine power, now evil.

My heart pounded at high speed and I tensed as I watched them. I wished I had my friends with me. But I was alone.

Death would fill the streets tonight. Vampire blood would be spilled as the gates of Hell had been opened. All the damned were crawling through, feasting on the souls of men and vampires and destroying their hearts.

I wanted time to heal after that genocide, after fighting in the conflict. For a while, at least I gained some kind of peace...I'd forgotten I was sleeping whilst I was dreaming; surreal images and feelings flooded my mind. But now I realised that in the realm of the supernatural, nothing rests for long...

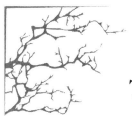

The Crypt.

Anthony

I GASPED IN SHOCK, the cold air jolting me into consciousness.

Open your eyes. Open them! But I could not. It took several pain-staking minutes, and then even longer for my vision to adjust.

As my eyes strained in that dark place, I found myself lying on an earthen floor in a dusty, mildewed crypt. I shuddered as cold from the frozen floor penetrated through my clothes into my body. My stiff frame was reluctant to move so I started by moving my hands and feet. Pain seized my body.

Short and rasping breaths, my lungs were chilled. I thought my body was stronger than this, but as my memory returned I realised I had gone to ground during autumn and it now felt like deep winter.

Ice encrusted the ivy growing over the sarcophagus in the crypt and a trickle of fear crept inside my stomach as my mind made sense of the situation that I had fled from. And now my mind pulled together the past events that had led me to hiding out here in the first place.

5

I remembered my not too distant past when I had been happy, mortal, and living an ordinary life. I'd had a job that I liked, and a girlfriend who loved me, introverted and introspective as I was. I glanced over to her. She looked so peaceful sleeping at my side that you could be forgiven for thinking she was dead. I'd had all the normal trappings of human existence and had been ignorantly happy.

My body jolted involuntary as the memory of the night that changed my life flooded back.

The thugs, the vampires that drained me to near death, then forced me to drink their fetid blood. They were not dashing and bold, they were vile, demonic, and without language. Their stench alone was repulsive. But my instinct, my will to survive kicked in, and I had gulped their blood fast. Things went to Hell in a matter of months.

As I lay there thinking, body rigid from the cold in that grey crumbling grave, slowly able to digest the changes that had been thrust at me. I had killed innocent humans in the beginning. My body thrust the mercy of the lashing torrent of blood lust. My soul severed from my consciousness.

Before being vampire, I wouldn't harm a thing. And the memory of that innocent woman still haunted me. Little had I known at the beginning that killing innocents was forbidden. Little had I realized that my past evils would torment me forever.

Then I'd joined with other vampires succumbing to debauchery, preying on criminals...I was an unstoppable force. The hunger drove me with an urgency that I was incapable of controlling. Then I was dragged into the crazy ideology of a despot Elite vampire war. Their mission to rid the world of the lower orders of vampires, creating an army of vampires genetically enhanced with the Elite genes to rule and govern the underworld.

I had found myself locked up, chained up, and bled and beaten before being altered further by my vampire *friend*. I was lucky to escape with my life.

As these memories streamed into my mind, my body tensed and breathing quickened. I took a slow, deep breath. I was glad to have time to realise how much I'd survived and how much I'd changed.

But what am I now? A killer. A drinker of human blood. I drank the blood of a demi-god, by her choosing, to save my life. I had been infected by a creature made by the Elite. An experimental. Neither vampire nor human, he'd undergone the gene therapy to turn it into an Elite soldier. It didn't work on everyone, and those whose physiology rejected the genes were mutated into something hideous into a state of limbo, unable to take blood or food. The demi-god, Emidius, saved me with her blood after I was bitten trying to kill the crazed beasts. She told me that she saw potential in me.

What that is I have no idea, unless it is my charming personality and my extensive DVD collection. She who everyone feared, what was she really? I have no idea.

My name is Anthony and I have been a vampire for a few years and now I want nothing more than to live as I did before I was a vampire. I cannot, I know. But I want to return to life and blend effortlessly into the background. I want to live with Rachel, my lover who was turned by my vampire friend. Selfish, yes. But she came willingly, her choice made mostly by the danger of the growing amount of vampires prowling in the city.

So after all that, I went to ground with her. I had no clue actually that I could do this, it was instinct. And fear. Even though I knew I had more power than most thanks to Emidius for sharing her blood. I had wanted to get away from the fall out of the Elite's failed eugenics programme and war.

And Rachel. She thought she had killed her maker and my friend, Nathaniel. But he was old and strong and I *knew* he still lived. Though God knows how as he was doused in petrol and set on-fire after she drove a fire poker into him.

Closing my eyes for a second, I rested whilst images of that night flooded my mind with a million other thoughts. My thoughts chattered at me like birds greeting the dawn. My body started to revive and I could feel my limbs willing to be moved. Slight warmth moved gently through my body and breathing was less laboured.

Hiding in crypts in 2017. I spat a laugh at the irony of it. Who knew! And I was dressed in black. I must have been born to it!

My eyes opened slightly wider now and I looked again over at my lover. She was like an effigy, pale and cold to touch. Like death. Fitting for this timeworn place. Inside the crypt lay a few crumbling sarcophagi and frosty creepers twisted around them mixed with moss. Like something from a macabre tale.

Slowly, I sat up and felt my back ease as I moved it. I was rigid from lying still for so long and the freezing cold. Looking at my hands, they shimmered as frost had covered them and my body. On Rachel it gave the illusion of an ice queen. Gradually I stood up, blood rushing through my legs, heat reviving them.

As I stepped outside, a surge of energy rose in my body, rousing my senses. Everything was so acute—the air sweet with the scent of rotting leaves and the crisp chill of the wind on my face. Stronger than before and connected to this earth like no other. This sensation was new to me. My feet were ground to the floor as if I truly were a part of this wild nature, herself.

The cold air made my breath look like the smoke from a dragon's mouth and a small stream of light peaked through to the back of this dank place where we lay hidden, forgotten. Dreaming.

I stretched and saw that day was parting now, just as winter had left the surrounding woods bare of their thick autumn greenery. Scents and colours, warm and vivid, it was bliss.

I remembered a sensation then, such an unusual feeling as I had left Nathaniel's charred remains. The sense of being watched by something that I did not know or understand. But something that told my instincts to fear and to remember. A shiver ran over me, and I blinked quickly. Yes, something powerful and deadly. I slumped a bit at the thought. No, we would remain low key.

Nathaniel. I could feel him. I had drunk his blood. His genes had been mixed with mine. He was part of me and I knew he lived. I closed my eyes to breathe in his memory, his passion for life.

Though he had terrified Rachel, wicked and evil as he is, I was excited to know he was out there. My desire to see him was strong and I found myself thinking how heartless I must be, to long for the creature who could have killed my lover. But no more, as I had more strength than him.

In the beginning, I thought of him as a friend, a confidant. And he still was in his own fiendish way. Maybe my feelings towards his friendship were in part because it was him who had saved me at the beginning of this nightmare, or at least I thought he had. Before him, I was alone and terrified with this transformation of horror, and he had befriended me. And again, when destiny led me to a fate worse than death at the hands of the Elite, it was him that saved me. I didn't trust him, but I did miss him.

An unsettling and strange power surged within me. It was a bit like wearing a new coat; I liked it but I didn't fit it yet. Cumbersome but warm.

Emidius, it was said, was thousands of years old and protective of her fragile humans. To have her blood changes you, keeps you out of reach of humanity, and I had started to sense this.

Having seen the brutality of other vampires, I was determined not to succumb to that.

Wandering back into the crypt, I took one last deep breath, trying to drive away the darkness that haunted my soul. If the Elite found me now, I'd have to face them, but I was done with this. This was not living, and living is what I wanted now more than anything.

I found myself stooping over Rachel, her pale face and pink lips, an ethereal beauty. As I bent to kiss her a powerful yearning stirred in me. She awoke to find me drinking on her slender neck.

She sighed and I unlatched my teeth, looked at her, and grinned a bloody grin. Then I took her blood again and as my teeth sunk into her flesh, my passion awoke. As I drank from her I thought of all the people who I had bled, of my debauched past. It was as if my passion and blood lust were automated, animalistic and now I hated that. That as a vampire I cannot have one without the other. I wondered if she felt the same. Vampires, emotionally cold. Driven by sensation. It reminded me of a quote from Dorian Gray. He sought pleasure but that is not the same as happiness.

Rachel was the lover I had lived with, but she was not the same person now that she was a vampire. I listened to the pounding of her heart, and felt her emotion travel through me as her blood touched my lips, my tongue, and my throat. That incurable addiction. Blood is more intimate than sex. That sharing, the emotions and the knowledge coming from the giver, no secrets.

Covered in filth, the lust that had lain dormant came back like a force of nature.

"I love you, I missed you," I told her as I grabbed her and held her close looking into her eyes, as lovers do. Searching for something more than lust, something deeper.

That kiss was powerful, Rachel with me and our blood mixed in our bodies, we were enraptured and my previous cold thoughts evaporated in an instant.

Now I felt connected like no other. I forgot about that feeling, that emotion about *outside*, about needing to be in life. Emotion is a powerful force. So I had answered my own question. I did feel deeper, emotionally connected, but I knew not all vampires did.

She was mine and I hers and the bond between us through blood and love felt unbreakable. Intense.

"Anthony," she whispered her voice dry. "I don't want to lose you again."

"You won't, I promise."

Maybe we had transcended from lust to something else, something stirring, something profound. I hoped so. I hoped it wasn't just *me* feeling this. Falling for an illusion like I had done so many times before.

Love is so consuming, so erotic no words could be spoken.

That night, we made love, laughing, loving, caressing. Until now, I hadn't known that was even possible as a vampire.

For three months, we'd slept in that dark crypt, arriving in autumn, and now the signs of winter had come I couldn't even remember when I last showered. But that hardly mattered. I'd just stay here with her and we would drink each other dry.

We lay there, like true children of the night, listening to the owls screeching and the foxes wailing in the distance. Bitter winds chilled my cold body more, but emotions inside me burned like a furnace. Nothing ventured near us and only the sounds of nature surrounded us. Dirty and dusty, we were happy.

Laying together in each other's arms, on that soil floor, watching the shadows chase across the ceiling as the light moved and bounced around I felt peaceful. If it wasn't for the hunger, I believe we could've stayed there indefinitely and just let the time of man pass us by and come out in maybe fifty years. But the hunger did start. Once awoken, it rages within our bodies like tidal waves, rushing on us and leaving us heady and dazed until we get our next fix. The blood of another vampire quickens us, but unless that vampire is powerful, it ceases to sustain us. My head spun and I felt disorientated. It was time to re-join the world.

What we would find out there we could only guess, so reluctantly we left our earthy haven and made the long walk back to civilisation.

But living; life yearned for me. Gripped by anticipation to return with Emidius's blood in my veins, stronger than ever and my lover by my side. With that precious elixir my body, mind, and heart forever changed, wielding a power unmatched by my kin. I had felt that confidence growing inside me. Not designed for sedentary life, the mundane.

We ran mile after mile and I was determined to start over a new leaf, not to steal a life or a car this time.

"I wonder what we'll find back home, who's left. You know, Nathaniel refused to help you when you and Jamie went back to the Elite to destroy them," Rachel spluttered.

"I saw him leave with you." As I said that, her eyes widened and her mouth fell open. Before she could say any more I added, "Rachel, I had to make a choice. It's not because I don't care. If we didn't destroy the Elite, there would be nothing, we wouldn't be here now. Believe me, I would have rather been with you."

Pausing a moment for the words to settle I continued, "Jamie and I took a bomb, two actually, made by a resistance group. We killed Tyrell, that mad leader and his foul son, Alexander. Actually, Tyrell lived through the bombing, but Jamie cut off his head! God it was gruesome, but appropriate. Then we hunted those things, the Experimentals. I was bitten by one, we failed in killing any, and Jamie took me to Emidius. Her blood saved me. Though she was insistent that Jamie could've done that."

"What of Jamie?"

"'The last I saw was Emidius looking for him. He wanted to be with her, he was sick of being a vampire, sick of taking orders from Tyrell and killing the lesser immortals. Other than that, I don't know. I recovered, I came to find you, I sensed where you were, we went to ground. I don't know anymore."

The silence between us wasn't unsettling, it was peaceful. We ran again together. We had both changed beyond imagining from our human existence. Life would never be the same.

Eventually we arrived in Bath. As the Elite had been less interested in Rachel, I thought her home would be safer for us to stay. Her tiny Georgian terrace home on the outskirts of the city was musty and cold from the months we'd been away. Mail had piled up so we had to shove the door open. As we plugged in our phones they buzzed with missed calls, all out of date by now. After switching on the heating to get rid of the musty smell and warm up, I went upstairs in search of a much needed shower. I had no clothes to change into so I chucked the filthy rags into the wash. We feel the cold, being sensitive to everything—noise, light and weather.

We logged onto the net to check the news to see if there were any unusual stories related to Tyrell and found a story about the complex that the Elite had used as their HQ. The building that Jamie and I had blown up. Of course the news was false and reported the explosion due to faulty gas mains. Plausible I guess, because the site was very old. I suspect that other members of the Elite vampires gave that report to the media. I know enough to believe they have a powerful empire around the world.

I had a ton of unanswered messages and emails from family and friends. My stomach felt heavy answering these. I had to lie. I lied that I had been called away as a close friend had been ill, though I guess it wasn't so far from the truth. I hated lying, especially to family and the few close friends who'd been brave enough to try and maintain contact. But what else could I do? For the time I shared with them, in their mortal existence, having to lie made the breach even wider.

I heard nothing from my vampire friends. I had expected something from Jamie. Our friendship had been short, but we had been through Hell together. I hoped he was alright. Maybe he wasn't even a vampire now.

As I wandered into the living room, Rachel blurted out, "I had a dread about the payments for my home, my bills, but it seems they're all up to date. And I just checked my bank statement and it says I'm twenty-seven thousand pounds in credit. Where the Hell did that come from?"

I knew the answer to that and I knew she'd hate it. And I had to tell her...

"When Nathaniel turned you, when he stayed with you, he set up a fund for you. You know he's wealthy, you don't know how rich he is. He made you, he saw it as his duty to protect you. Things, as you've seen, get out of hand when you enter the paranormal world and having a base, a home to flee to is important. I know you're probably pissed off about that, but really, he cared. He just wasn't stable. Something happened to him in his past that tipped his mental state. I don't know what. But anyway, that's why you're fine."

She didn't say a word. I could tell by her stern expression she was angry but at the same time, without his help, she may not have had a house to come back to. He was unbalanced, that's putting it mildly, but going from human to vampire isn't exactly the easiest trick for anyone to pull off. I would know. Any weakness seems highlighted. Any deviance becomes exaggerated.

"Any news?" I asked.

"Family, friends, work...all good stuff. Nothing macabre. Thank God."

We closed up the computers and went to get dressed. My clothes were washed and dried, though shabby from the time in the crypt. Then we were ready to head out into the city to merge into society again, and it felt odd being so completely surrounded by humans.

Even before our sleep, I had only kept the company of vampires for a long time and I had forgotten what it was like to be surrounded by mortals. Staring at them with their drinks and their carefree living, laughing, relaxing. I envied them. Life is so easy for them. They have innocence about them. They are like children, deceived, misguided and susceptible. I wanted that.

I remembered when I had thought briefly I could've been turned back to human by the Elite, and that was an interesting idea though not possible. There had been reports of the Elite's genetics plan. They were in fact breeding an army of vampires by splicing the genes from the Elite and injecting these into the lost souls they thought fit for carrying out their orders. Gene therapy not used much in human medicine and for good reason. Nathaniel had saved me, having his genes infused into me. I think that's why he has such a hold over me. I am now part of him.

I wondered at the lengths Tyrell had gone to, to breed his Elite army of immortals before Jamie removed his head. "Ah, Jamie, I guess you're with Emidius now?" I mused.

I ran my fingers through Rachel's hair. She looked good enough to eat! We stood in a small, crowded bar, so close to humans. I loved their smell. It intoxicates me and makes me feel wild. Intentionally, I stand close, envious of their mortal existence, their life that is not driven by blood-lust. So fragile, so pure, even the nastiest humans are, to me, so frail.

Sometimes a thought will rush into my mind; *I could just drag them off and drink them. But I don't.*

And so we stood there looking like them with our untouched drinks in our hands. It came to me then the reason I felt so disturbed.

I would have to teach her how to hunt. Humans. She'd only ever drank the blood of immortals so far and I don't think it had even occurred to her that she would have to drink a living human's blood. I would teach her to drink only evil doers. She had drunk the blood of her Maker and of me. It sustains us but we cannot thrive on it. Only human blood can do that. As she had been changed in haste during the Elite war, then captured, she hadn't spent any time with mortals. She had been held captive by Nathaniel at the Elite's complex, my being unable to be with her due to Tyrell's evil campaign. I had entrusted her safety to Nathaniel, who I had also injured, but that is another tale…

When I was first changed, I had almost bled her dry. And after her I had killed innocents. I couldn't tell Rachel this. I couldn't bear the way she would look at me if I told her that. She would see me as a heartless murderer. Which of course, I was. My first kill. I would tell her about that in time, a long, long time in the future. But for now, for tonight, we would head home and I would try and put this out of my mind.

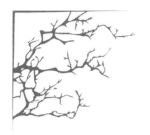

Marcus

Anthony

HIS PRESENCE WAS LIKE a nightmare. His great wings beating slowly, he was a sublime manifestation. Crouching on top of a small Georgian terraced house, near Rachel's home, he looked more animal in his stance. Not human.

His eyes followed Rachel and the slight upturn of his lips gave away his intention towards her. His thoughts seemed to muddle inside my mind and I realised he was in my head. Standing up slowly he then jumped to the ground softly, pulling in his huge black feathered wings. As he stepped towards us, instinctively my body tensed, my mouth parched whilst adrenalin pumped like wildfire.

We faced each other eye to eye, my feet planted, heart racing, and heat flushing through me. Silence echoed around us, wispy shadows flickering on buildings under the slight moon light. The only sounds our breathing.

One more step towards us and Rachel gasped, making me jump instinctively.

Lunging forward, I threw all my power at him, but he laughed and made no effort to push me aside. His expression changed when he realised he'd underestimated me and staggered back a few steps, his mouth dropping open, his arms flayed and then a huge grin appeared. He grabbed my arm, I struggled, bringing my other arm up to punch him, jerking my body back at the same time. The death grip on my arm didn't allow me to move though. I felt like a child or a fish as I wriggled from the end of the fishing line. I wasn't going anywhere. My grunted curses were cut short as the winged man spoke. I looked up to see Rachel speechless and motionless, terror etched on her beautiful face. My anger was quickly morphing into hatred as I saw her fear, but at that moment, I was powerless to do anything but listen.

"I don't want to fight you. I have come to ask for your help." His voice sounded preternaturally deep and echoed around the buildings.

In place of anger, cold fear ran through my body. My throat dry, I swallowed hard. I forced my words out of my mouth. "Leave, whatever the hell you are!" I didn't want this. The supernatural world was bigger than I could imagine and every time I went out something crept out of the shadows to bring its messed up world into mine. Or so it seemed.

We stood in a face off. He was not backing down, so I took Rachel's hand to leave. He made no effort to stop us and I never looked back.

I wanted our life back and I was determined to get it.

I heard him inside my mind again, calling me. I stopped abruptly and turned towards him. He had followed us, but the lightness of his step meant that I hadn't heard him.

"What? What is it that you need *my* help with? You seem powerful—more powerful than me. So what use can I possibly be to you?"

"I was searching for Emidius. I cannot find her. You have her blood in you, so you can help me." He tilted his head the way an animal does when it is listening.

I had no idea what the feathered man was. He looked human, but didn't act human. His actions, his movements were animalistic.

"Help you find her? I doubt it. If she chooses not to be found, I cannot do a damn thing about that. Why are you looking for her? Who are you?" The words spewed forth.

"I have been watching you." I noticed then that his slate grey eyes had no whites, they were solid grey and I sensed an ancient power.

My gut was tight. Rachel had not spoken a word and I thought she was fascinated by this ethereal vision by the fact that she looked awe struck, her eyes beaming. My instinct told me to be careful, that although my strength is increased, I needed to be wary of his.

He seemed to have some air of divine presence about him, but also something darker, something menacing. His skin was slightly tanned and his features, though perfectly symmetrical, were large, like him. Big velvety eyes, high cheek bones, and mouth slightly too big for his face. Wearing just jeans and a hoodie, his body was lean and stealthy. Wild, dark hair. And those massive black feathered wings. What was he?

His voice was so deep and reverberating. "My name is Marcus. I'm not a vampire but a nephilim. My kind hates vampires. In fact, we spend our time hunting you down and killing you.

To us, your kind is a vermin to humanity, taking human blood, killing them. I grew bored of the slaughter and after three-hundred years, I wanted to taste something different from life. I made that decision in a heartbeat, and that changed everything.

"I tasted vampire blood. I am the only one of my kind. As I'm sure you know, nephilim blood is lethal to vampire kind although it is, so I hear, divine." He said this last part with a smirk. "But that doesn't mean that vampire blood was lethal for my kind. Nobody'd tried it, and I changed that. Nobody had been brave enough, until me. Until now..."

He paused here and took another step forward. My heart skipped a beat and my stomach tightened even more. He was going to drink us?

In the deathly silence we stood amongst the compact nineteenth century houses on the edge of the city. We stood there in silence for several minutes, and not a soul passed. I felt cold from the cloudless sky and brisk wind. Marcus radiated a cool aura which chilled me further. I watched him. He stood there in the moonlight like a mythical character that had stepped straight from the pages of a fable, his breath coming out in steaming puffs. He continued his tale when neither Rachel nor I responded...

"Now I am hunted by vampire and nephilim alike. I am a new breed. A hybrid. I am damned by God, damned by my own kind, and damned by those I hunted. And so I fled here, to this small city to find the demi-god, Emidius. But I cannot find her so I sought out the one saved by her. When I find her, I will drink her blood. I hope it will restore my place, my connection with God and allow me to reinstate my soul. But I can find only you.

"You are powerful in your own right. You who hid for months, yet you were strong enough to wipe out the Elite. You drank from demons and survived their venom. You are much stronger than you think, and even more so with the blood of Emidius running through your veins.

"I must restore myself to my former glory. I have never fallen foul to debauchery. I am from pure angelic blood, from the essence of God and my blood has been tainted by that of an impure vampire. With this blood, I am experiencing uncontrollable rage and hatred, lust and desire. I wish to purge myself of these impurities. I must not be ruled by the blood of the underworlders that run through my veins."

Before we could answer, he continued, "I need companions. I know enough that I cannot survive this on my own. I had thought I would find Emidius. She at least would no doubt find my predicament diverting and could help me. I left the North, I left before my kin found out. Before they realised that I had stopped before I killed a hapless vampire, scanned its macabre face. I hunted many that night and killed them all, except this one. I had long ago locked out the wailing cries of lesser immortals; it could have been saying anything. But as I stopped and looked at it, it was female. It was angry and it was scared. Its face was contorted from screaming. I have rarely known fear." He paused.

"We nephilim never spoke to those inferior to ourselves. We are a proud race and our anger surpasses all beings, except that of a demi-god. I scanned my victim's face searching for clues, clues as to what life felt like to be a vampire. I took her head easily with one hand and tilted it to the side. I could hear her heart beating so fast, pumping. Pumping that evil elixir that held a thousand souls or more, for this one had lived a long time. And I knew then that there would be no turning back. This would determine my fate. I have lived so long, a celestial being in grace. And now, finally, I gave into temptation in the guise of a vampire, or was this really the Devil? Did her blood really hold the souls of the dead? I put my teeth over her artery and bit gently at first. It was odd but easy, within seconds that corrupt fluid flowed its way into me. Once I started I couldn't stop. The creature let out a pathetic wail as it slumped to the ground and I stood there swaying."

He continued, his tale spilling forth in a flurry with no thought to breathe between sentences. "As the infected blood rushed through my veins, then too late I prayed. The sudden comprehension of my error dawned and I begged God for mercy. What have I done? I was terrified, shock sweeping over me and I fell to my knees and convulsed, my wings now with the sinister poison in them, turned from pure white to black! My life, my purpose, my mission flew before me in a mass of swirling confusion.

"I vomited—so strange. I had never had *any* illness. Then I passed out where I was next to the dead vampire. When I awoke with a pain so severe and was horrified to find the mess that *I* had made. A thousand thoughts whisked in my mind all at once. I had been tempted, and now it was too late, spiralling to the depths of Hell with the blood of a fiend in my body! I had committed the worst crime of my kind. In fact, it has never been documented that any nephilim had drunk the blood of a vampire. For a vampire to drink the blood of the nephilim was considered the worse crime of all. But I had just created a new crime more heinous than that!" He started laughing somewhat hysterically.

I was dumbfounded. It was too absurd, too surreal. His low ethereal voice boomed with pain of his own disbelief.

"What had I been thinking? Surely this was some evil hex, a spell that something more powerful than I had cast. And now the weight of the situation fell upon me. I got up unsteadily knowing I should go and confess to my elders. But if I confessed, death would ensue followed by an eternity of torment in oblivion with all those terrible souls that I myself had cast there. No. I must leave and fast. I needed to clean myself, but I was too heavy to move, to fly. For the first time in my life, my wings weighed me down, my body dense with that unholy blood of a vampire."

Rachel and I stood there in bewilderment as this fallen angel told us his life story, spewing it all out. I wanted him to leave as I sensed a threat from him. But I was too transfixed by his tale, by him. I had so many questions.

"As I walked to the place I called home, the humans around me looked at me with disgust, crossing the road to avoid me. It was terrible, none of this was normal. I felt strange as that blood flowed inside me and awoke with it a carnal yearning that I had never known. I need your help. You are the only ones who can help me, at least until I find Emidius."

"I can only tell you where I last found her, hidden from the world in a cave. But whether or not she's still there, I don't know. Others may know. If I can't find her, what will you do then? You cannot stay with us; your own kin will no doubt be hunting you." I was adamant that I would not accept him.

Rachel added, "It is too dangerous for you to stay here. We know only a few of our kind, the others." She looked at me. "Jamie? Maybe he's with her, he could help."

I nodded. She was right. If anyone knew where she was it would be Jamie. Last time I'd seen him he'd walked away from Emidius, but she had gone after him. I still had his number.

"I can call him and ask, but you need to find somewhere to stay. You cannot stay with us."

"I swear to you that I will see to it that no harm comes to either of you. If my kin come here, the only creature that could save you from them is a nephilim. No other could protect you. You don't seem to know much about us," he added rather shocked that we didn't know.

"We don't, no." I looked at Rachel who looked pale in shock. "We will help you, but you're asking too much to come into our home."

"It would only be for tonight, please? I don't want to be alone." He paused and looked uneasy. "As hard as this is for me to admit, I am afraid. Lonely, scared. I have no others."

Rachel said, "But how can we trust you?"

"Rachel," he said trying to keep his intense voice quiet and soft and not succeeding, "If I wanted your blood, I could have already taken it. And it tempts me, it does to be honest. But I need your help more. I am a fool, but not foolish enough to harm those who are my only hope of survival." He dropped his head, looking resigned to his hopeless position.

Not long ago he would have killed us for being what we are, but fate often has a sense of humour, and so he had to beg the help of those he'd despised for hundreds of years.

"You are right; I can't survive without you. I apologise, I can't stop from hearing your thoughts. What I can promise, however, that should my kin come I will protect you and I won't impose too much on your life," he added quickly, his voice resonating through me. Somehow I doubted that, but I tried not to think it.

I knew there was no point in arguing, As cold as I felt, I couldn't turn him away, I remembered when I was first a vampire and how relieved I was when Nathaniel took me under his wing. My instincts told me he was sincere, but they also told me that trouble would be right behind him. No chance of a quiet existence!

He was locked into an existence by one mistake. My mistake had been to ignore the vagrants that night long ago that ended up viciously turning me.

I felt an empty resignation as we led the way back to her place. Rachel made it clear that this was for one night only. That he could stay here tonight, but he needed to find a place tomorrow.

Despite our not wanting him in our home, his reluctance to be here, his displeasure with our modest home, angered me more. I reminded myself though that the more displeased he was, the faster he'd leave. I guessed he was used to something grander.

We had received no response from Jamie. I texted him, emailed, and called but his phone just went to voicemail. I knew Marcus wanted to find Emidius before he yielded into drinking blood, and so the next day we headed out of Bath towards North Bristol to Goblin Combe where I had last seen her.

The place was bare with winter, leafless branches reaching down to the ground like skeleton arms and bony hands ready to grab any passer-by. Crunching through the woodland, icy ground sparkled in the sunlight. I had wanted to leave early afternoon so I had some light to recognise the opening, to remember whereabouts we had found near the entrance to the cave that was cut into the gorge. Jamie found it by tuning into his intuition, so I tried the same. The woodland around was extensive, but it was easy enough to find the gorge.

The gorge was majestic surrounded by woodland then rolled downhill gently, lush green farmland, it was a place of spectacular beauty. Rachel and Marcus fell silent as we wandered around. It didn't take long to find it, remembering the sights and the rock face from before. The entrance was narrow and deep and most of all dark. Rachel had the foresight to bring a torch. Although we had exceptional vision, caves are darker than night and the pitch blackness was difficult and unsettling.

Squeezing through the gap, concentrating on our footing we, one by one, stepped in and followed the narrow path into the earth. As I remembered it was cold and black, but most of all I didn't sense another being inside. Our path was slippery, and we clung to the walls as the tight tunnel and unstable footing made it difficult. Poor Marcus, as big as he was, found it especially hard.

"You found her here?" Marcus questioned, his voice raised.

"I did. I don't sense anyone here now, but maybe there'll be a clue?"

We found our way into a pitch black cavern and Rachel turned on the torch.

"Over here," my voice echoed around the empty chamber making me smirk. "She had been in this part when we found her." As I looked around an adjacent hollow it was clear that she was long gone. But I was determined to find something, some clue as to how to contact her.

"Why the hell would she live in a cave if she's so powerful?" Rachel spoke as bewildered as Marcus.

"I think she liked to be close to the Earth and away from humanity. That I can understand," I answered.

"For sure, but why not live in a house, or cabin far away. A cave? It's pretty primitive!"

"Well, I had heard that she is thousands of years old. When Jamie and I came here, this part that we're in now, it was lit and it looked warm and inviting, although I never got to see it myself. I saw it from over there. I'd been bitten by that half vampire, half zombie creature of Tyrell's. Jamie brought me here for her to help me, and he in turn wanted to stay with her. He was tired of Tyrell's war on lesser vampires and tired in general of immortals and their petty wars. They argued, he left. She gave me her blood and then followed him. I haven't heard from him to this day, so I don't know what happened to either of them. But she seemed fond of him. I was hoping to find some clue here, something to help you."

But I didn't. The smaller cavern where Emidius had emerged from was empty, as if no one had ever been here. "I'm going to scout the area, though if there was any evidence it's probably long gone."

"Can't you just call for her? Isn't that what the others did?" Rachel asked.

Marcus added solemnly, "She is of a different era. No nephilim has ever done that. We revere her only because she brought some order to the chaos of the vampires and their like. Her magic is unlike mine. It is pagan whereas mine is, or was, divine. It was a chance I was hoping for, though whether or not she would've helped was a gamble. Don't worry Anthony, I think it is clear that she isn't to be found and neither is your friend. They are gone. They could be literally anywhere."

Marcus sighed, his head hung low, and he slouched. Avoiding eye contact, I saw his lips were pressed tightly. Rachel, seeing this was quick to act, reminding me of one of the reasons I loved her—her compassion for others.

"Look, you can stay with us until you sort out a place of your own. I won't say live because who knows where you truly want to be. You need to take stock. You are not alone—we are here. Maybe your kin are hunting you, so now you need to consider a plan. And afterwards, how will you live? I understand the comfort of being rescued by one stronger than you, but now you have to rescue yourself. But as I said, you're not alone. What will you do with the life you have chosen? The consequences of your decisions have led to this point. What you must decide now is what to do with that." She rubbed his arm for comfort, and smiling turned to me.

"Let's go home, we'll find nothing here. I fear for Jamie, but maybe he's with her living something we can't comprehend." And laughing, she added, "And maybe he doesn't need mobile phones, texting now. Maybe he's doing something more incredible!"

So I drove us back.

It was cumbersome having Marcus in Rachel's home. He was exaggerated in everything he did and his voice sounded so loud and his expressions were extravagant.

Our little home seemed too small to contain him and it felt like he would burst out of it like a jack in the box. As he sat splayed out on the sofa he took up all of it. I felt some angst at that point that I now had to live with this colossus of a man, with my girlfriend, and he looked like a model. I do not. He was enough to intimidate most men.

Immediately hearing my thoughts, he chuckled, face surprised as if he didn't realise this. Modest then.

As the days went on and he stayed with us, unable to find somewhere fast, I considered letting him use my flat, at least that way Rachel and I could have some privacy. Although he was graceful, his presence and size made me claustrophobic.

I watched him as he helped around the house, his manner towards us ever polite. He slept in the spare room, though it couldn't have been too comfortable as the spare bed was a single and he was so big. But his gratitude shone. I think he was relieved not to be alone.

After just two days, I knew I had to take him out to hunt, he was horrified to realise that he had to drink the blood of humans, even evil doers. Due to his celestial heritage he hadn't given into his vampiric thirst since the one he drained. He had bargained for Emidius to help him so that he wouldn't have to do that. He had fought the thirst with all of his nephilim might.

Emidius certainly cured me when I had been bitten by the infected creature, and even now I still felt her power throbbing through me. Whether or not she had the power to change Marcus, I had no idea. They both seemed to come from different traditions, but one thing I've learned in this paranormal world is that there is often some truth in legends and tales.

Marcus believed vehemently that blood contained the soul of the person. On telling me this, I shuffled around, and to say this concept made me uncomfortable was putting it mildly.

If that's true, had I taken the souls from all my victims? That was something I didn't want to consider.

And now I had to help Rachel, who up until now had only drunk the blood of other vampires, mainly Nathaniel's and mine. It had been enough to sustain her but it wouldn't be enough in the long term.

Vampires only *exist* on each other's blood, and we need human blood to live, to thrive.

So I had to guide him through the process and at the same time teach Rachel.

I felt like a parent, though to give Rachel her due she didn't resist as much as I think she would have, if I not had Marcus to contend with as well. As I talked to them about this, she fidgeted, her mouth turning downwards whilst Marcus, his eyes wide with shock, just stared at me in horror.

But once Marcus had the taste, he had become a force, righteous in his new found role of protector of the innocent. The hunger, once tasted, drives us with little control.

The park was silent in those winter nights, though fortunately for us some malcontents still roamed around looking for victims. How ironic that they looked to commit crime and yet we found them. Karma perhaps...

When he approached his victims, Marcus was able to read their minds which turned him into a torrent of fury. I had to hold him back—no easy task—to stop him from killing them all, and his thirst, once awoken, never seemed quenched. Aside from the inconvenience of killing every victim, he would be left with consequences of morality that would haunt him, should he kill. I knew that from experience.

Rachel was more discreet, but filled with disgust that she had to feed on the blood of rapists and abusers. The fact that she had to put her lips to their corrupt flesh and drink their foul blood repulsed her, but this was quickly overcome once the elixir filled her body.

Under the barren trees they fed remorselessly and Marcus became more aggressive and beyond control. The effect on his physiology was harsh, sending him thrashing to the ground in a fit of pain mixed with the pleasure of satisfying his thirst. Calming him down was a feat in itself. I had to make him get it together, aside from the noise and attention we needed to be able to blend in. He was so dramatic.

I looked on, ever aware that such scenes would be noticed. Fortunately I never came across anyone else. A mixture of guilt and pride filled me as I looked on at my lover, seeing the power grow within her, the dark vampiric changes. Her strength was increasing, but unlike me in the beginning she was strong and held true to her morals and humanity.

Though I had little time to think my own thoughts and with one who could read my mind when he was in close vicinity of me, I was glad.

Where ever we went, humans were drawn to us, but I was keen to blend in.

You may wonder how the hell does a nephilim blend in with wings? And you'd be right to ask that question. But when he chose, though now it was apparently harder than before the blood, he could turn his wings invisible to all those but the very enlightened or other supernaturals. I didn't believe it myself, I confess, and I cringed as I watched him walk ahead of us into a bar. But to my amazement, no one seemed to noticed. It was bizarre. Marcus, of course, was used to attention, but things got stranger pretty soon after.

This continued for some days and I was perturbed that Marcus was still unable to find his own place. It seems that he left in such a hurry, without identification and papers, that renting seemed impossible. And he now could no longer call upon his kin for help.

One morning, we were all listening to music relaxing in the lounge. The night had been long and all of us needed to take some time out. Rachel went upstairs to sleep, and I took the opportunity to ask him about his life before this. I was genuinely interested as I didn't know much about his kind, and I also wanted to know what else was out there that I didn't know about.

"Anthony, do you really want to know?" he asked grinning. "Or do you want to taste my blood? I only ask because I want to taste yours. Would that be something you would agree to?"

I was taken aback by his question, but he was brazen. Laughing, I said, "Of course I'm intrigued, but I don't want to die drinking your blood! Burnt from the inside out? No thanks...and as for you drinking mine, I've seen the way you take from the living. How would I know you wouldn't drain me dry? Contrary to your question, I do want to know your story. Where do you come from?"

"Alright... But I should start by telling you that not all nephilim are good. There are some, many in fact, that live in the shadows and are attracted to the darker things in life." He raised his eyebrows here as he realised that he was now talking about himself. "My early life was spent with my father protecting me from these most evil and foul creatures and teaching me how to fight. I grew up in Toulouse, France. I was born on 20th June, 1683; the year after the *Canal du Midi* was built.

"Some decades before my birth, plague devastated Toulouse twice. Most of the nobles had fled, but my father and others of our kind stayed to help. After all, it would not affect us. But plague attracts those who prey upon the sick and the weak and during my first few hundred years, evil roamed with an inexhaustible force. I know of late, the Elite vampires, like Tyrell, planned to eradicate the overpopulation of vampires that you were caught up in. But that was nothing compared with the past, my youth. In the past, the numbers of vampires was so widespread, like a pestilence upon all lands. And back then humanity was not as humane as it is now. Vampires today can be cruel, but in the past there were more that were savage. It seems many were unable to hold onto any benevolence.

"It was easier back then to kill and never be traced, and so they infected every corner of the planet. Today you have so many modern powers in place. Police, crime units, the internet. Everyone has a birth record, everything is detected. Your bank details, your phone calls. Remember in the seventeenth century people could go missing much easier? So much of my early life was spent with other nephilim killing the vampires and protecting the innocent human lives. Times were bloody, brutal, and filthy. Disease was everywhere and only wealth kept us from the foulness of life—poverty and crime."

Marcus paused here and looked thoughtful as he stretched back in remembering a time when living was harsh, deplorable, even for him.

"Death was closer to the living than it is now, at least in the Western world. If you travel to the poorer places now, you would, especially as a preternatural being, be aware that evil is ever-always waiting around the corner. It thrives. The past was crueller than you can imagine, Anthony. Grime. Humans lived in such conditions that even when we saved them from the horrors, often they would die of disease, of filth. Here, although evil lies here, it is minute compared to the past. Never lose sight of that, know that what you have now is so much better than your past."

As he sat there thinking, I paused to reflect on my own life, after all the madness that had come into my life before now. I used to like to drink coffee, my favourite food was Mexican, and I had enjoyed sharing meals with my human friends. Now my life had changed beyond recognition and I hadn't seen my family for nearly two years. We were never close and many, many months would elapse before seeing each other. I was closer to my friends than my family. But their most recent email to me had filled me with sadness knowing I could never see them again. They wanted to see me, but that was impossible. And my chest tightened just to think about it, they would fear me in the first few seconds of meeting me, subconsciously perhaps. And I couldn't have that.

I knew I was lucky; I had a lot to look forward to. I was after all sitting here with this creature that was over three hundred years old, and this was an extraordinary experience, but in the end I would trade that in an instant to go back to being mortal again.

"Life is easier today, and even though the paranormal world is thriving, it is at least under more control now than it was in the past. And as for people, their lives, their problems are easy compared to that of their ancestors. No longer in the West do you see the dying in the street, the dirt, the cruelty. Money is abundant for those willing to use their skills and talents, and this"—and here he held out his phone—"this technology is incredible. It is power and those who are willing to embrace it. In the past, no matter how much people wanted to better their lives, they were ruled by a rigid social structure. That no longer exists, here at least." Pausing, he sighed. "I don't wish to continue dwelling on the gloom of the past. The only thing that kept me driving forward was my mission to rid the world of underworlders and protect humanity.

"This city long ago was nothing like the city you live in today. You may or may not experience this for yourself if you live long enough. I won't lie to you, even for me it isn't an easy concept living so long, seeing the changes in humanity even though they are, in the main for the better. The past can haunt you if you're not strong enough to put it behind you." He shuffled in his seat and let out a sigh. "So, what now?"

"We rest. Tomorrow I'm going to go to my flat. I haven't been there in many, many months. I need something more to occupy my mind, more than blood."

"I see. There are other creatures circling around, have you not sensed them?"

"I have sensed something, yes. But I need some serenity. No offence."

He blurted out a short laugh, as if my wanting peace was incredulous. "So, you're an artist? I'd like to see what you do."

Marcus had the uncanny knack of pissing me off. The fact that he had invaded my mind, my privacy without permission. Before I could answer, he added quickly, "I'm sorry, I don't mean to pry. A habit, I do it without thinking and I have had little need in the past to apologise for this."

"Okay. Well, maybe I'll show you sometime. For now I just need to be alone for a bit. I never worked as an artist, I just create. If I was good at art, I would have a living from it. But what will *you* do next? I mean I can't imagine that you are going to be content staying with us, in Rachel's home. What did you do when you were not hunting my kind?"

"What, let you in on my secret?" He paused and I could sense he didn't want to talk about his private life. "Okay, as you have so graciously taken me into your lives, I see it only fitting that I let you into mine. And I do appreciate it. Without you two, I may be dead in the street by now, driven crazy by the insatiable hunger.

"When I need to have a break, I take a trip to Sardinia. I prefer the South and as it's a small island there's usually none or only a few immortals there. If there are any vampires, I either kill them or they leave me well alone. For me, being on a tiny island in the sun and the clear warm sea, I can forget myself. I spend my days reading, swimming, and diving. I like to mix and blend in and sometimes meet up with friends. I have a villa there; it's my home from home. I'd take you there, but I wouldn't want you to kill the locals. It's my sanctuary; it has been now for decades. I contemplated going there after this happened, but I feared I might rage out of control, and so needed to find someone to help me first."

"I can imagine that, a perfect place to forget. I guess that's what I need, Rachel *and* me. I like the fact you get away from other immortals. A place where I could create and be away from the others. It seems where ever immortals are, trouble follows fast. That annoys the hell out me."

He nodded an acknowledgment of that. It's as if being different from humans sends a beacon out, I would need to find a way to hide that beacon.

Before I left, another day passed and we slept soundly until night came. I convinced Rachel and Marcus to hunt together. I didn't need blood so often now and the craving was more psychological. Rachel looked unsure, but Marcus reassured her and I went off to my flat which I hadn't seen in nearly a year. Contradictory, I knew, as I had been jealous of Marcus, but now I knew he was trustworthy. I needed some time away and I would rather know she was safe with him than another. You never knew what was lurking in our paranormal world.

I had to go and sort out mundane tasks. Nathaniel had, in the past, shown me lucrative ways to make passive income, and along with his generosity, he'd also given me a very large sum of money.

When I got to my place and opened the door the smell was rancid. I had a ton of mail piled up, but funnily enough I felt a sense of ease just putting the heating on and sitting down and ploughing through all the letters, all the junk mail. Even vampires get junk mail! At least for the first century perhaps. I don't know, maybe forever!

Thoughts flooded back to when I was first turned and how Rachel had tried to help me at the very beginning of my change and how I nearly bled her dry. I felt a slight relief that even though that was heinous, I had somehow found the strength to stop myself from draining my girlfriend.

I wondered for a moment how Rachel and Marcus were getting on, but then my attention was drawn back to something in my flat. A faint sound from my bedroom. In an instant a shiver tingled down my spine, the hairs on my arms rigid. A slight familiar scent, though very faint, was in the air that I hadn't noticed when I first came in.

I knew then, I knew what I would find when I opened my bedroom door, but I didn't know the state he would be in.

And there he was huddled up on my bed, charred and bloody and burnt. Nathaniel.

Rachel had tried to kill him by dousing him in petrol after she'd plunged a fire poker through him. He *had* turned psychotic, which was why she had done it, but I also knew my treatment towards him had been wrong, too. I blamed myself. Had I treated him better he may have stayed stable, but too much had happened and all of us had lost our minds, our reason, very quickly. Not surprising under the circumstances being caught up in the war of the Elite. Nathaniel was an old and powerful vampire to be sure, but as he huddled there his vulnerability was prominent.

He didn't look up and slowly I went over to him and put my hand on his arm and just sat there.

At length he spoke, his voice strained, "I know I went crazy. When you turned on me, it reminded me of one I had loved long ago and whom I lost. That pain, it never healed, it only grew, it festered inside me." He took a huge breath, and his voice was strained. "I allowed Rachel to try and take my life. I'd suffered so long. Mortal loss never lessens over time. Unfortunately, it seems I cannot easily die." His voice was weak, laboured, and he made no eye contact. A small shrivelled version of the outgoing and confident vampire I had known before.

"I'm sorry for my part. It shouldn't have gotten to that. The madness of the eugenics project and taking down those in charge; we all lost control. And it looks like things aren't going to change either."

Nathaniel looked beyond help, fearful. It was clear that he was weak—too weak to feed, so I bit my wrist instinctively, knowing my powerful blood would help him but how much I couldn't be sure. He took it softly and as he drank I couldn't help but be horrified at his appearance. His once long, dark curly hair was no more. What was left was black and scorched. His skin was blackened and blistered. Being immortal, some healing had started, but the burning had been so intense that most of his skin hadn't grown back yet.

I sat on the bed close to him, my legs outstretched, and cradled his seared head in my lap whilst he drank from my wrist. He fell asleep almost straight away and I sat there watching over him. He was like a brother and he had, after all, in the beginning of my immortal existence, saved me.

I remember that so vividly. I was lost in fear of myself having just killed an innocent woman in the sways of bloodlust, beside myself with fear, fear of myself. Then he found me and became like a brother. God knows what I would have become without him.

After a while, I carefully moved him and pulled the covers over him whilst I went for a shower. I sent Rachel a text message to tell her I was fine but needed to stay away for a few days, but she didn't respond.

After a shower, I was pulling on some clean jeans when I had the oddest sensation of being watched, though there was clearly nothing in my flat with me, except Nathaniel who was sound asleep.

And nothing I could sense either, but still I felt eyes staring into me. A cold shiver ran through me. Not knowing whether or not it was my imagination or something real, I ignored it and went out. It was early in the morning now, around two-thirty and the streets were empty. I went to the largest park in the city to hunt after Nathaniel had taken my blood.

It, too, was oddly quiet, but I managed to find some vile excuse for a human. But what puzzled me was why the evil always smelled so bad? It was a thing. Their stench was like rotten bodies, I only noticed this now that I was immortal.

Having to alter his mind was a chore, but required less effort than burying a body. This one was particularly nasty and I was glad that I drank him almost dry so he had no chance of harming others. Changing the mentality of the damned was never too hard, for evil mortals are weak. If they were strong they wouldn't be evil—kind of a paradox for them. I left him believing he was unable to harm anything and to live humbly.

Back at my flat, Nathaniel was still sleeping and already started to look better. His skin, now a pinkish cream, was healing and the blisters fading. His breathing sounded smoother.

I grabbed a blanket and settled down on my sofa to rest, but that feeling of being watched came back. Something was unsettling and sinister. I tried to ignore it and shut my eyes, but the intensity of the feeling grew. Sensations of constriction an icy presence of death, maybe this was the fallout of Nathaniel's horrific experience, and I could sense it. I didn't know.

I tossed and turned, trying to block the impression. I punched the couch cushion to rid myself of the anger that this intruder was in my home and could unsettle me. That it was even here made me angry, yet all the turning and punching couldn't get rid of it. I finally stilled, choosing to ignore it, contenting myself in thinking that this presence was too cowardly to confront me directly. I finally fell asleep, but it wasn't restful.

I dreamt of some evil thing consuming Rachel, enveloping her and taking her away. but I only saw glimpses of how it looked, more I had a sense of its intention, wicked and spiteful. And she was lost to me and I was powerless to help her. A feeling of isolation and emptiness made me wake with a start and instinctively pull the blanket up around me. Sickness churned in my stomach and a cold sweat prickled across my skin. As I sat up, that presence had gone and it was warm in my home, but I still felt cold. Trying to find some normality, I looked at my phone. No messages.

I phoned her immediately, but again no answer so I phoned Marcus.

"Hey? You okay?"

"I don't know. Is Rachel there? Is she alright? She hasn't returned my messages. I was worried. I'm coming over."

"No need, just a minute." He spoke as quietly as was possible for him. "She's a bit pissed off, Anthony. You've been gone a few days; you should be with her. I get that you need your space, but you might get that permanently. I'm trying to keep her company."

"Okay, I think, thanks." I tried not to sound agitated by his answer.

I went to check on Nathaniel and give him more of my blood before heading back to Rachel. I'd take her out for the evening—not looking for blood, but somewhere different. The cinema or theatre. Then I could take her away for a week somewhere, like Marcus did with his bolt-hole. I knew it would do us good to get away, and I figured Marcus could by now look after himself for a bit. I might ask if we could go to his place.

"I'm leaving. I need to see Rachel, stay here and rest, I'll be back very soon."

He didn't speak. He took my blood and rested. His skin looked so much better, not a hundred percent, but clearer and his hair was growing back fast. I felt his strength as his mouth locked onto my wrist and I heard the pumping of my blood into him. He was starting to look more like himself.

Where Angels Tread

Anthony

AS I ARRIVED AT RACHEL'S home I found Marcus on the sofa reading. He sat up as I came in. "She's out, I'm afraid. I said you were coming!"

"What did she say?" Regret washed through me, and anger seeing him there and that was where I was supposed to be.

"Nothing and I tried not to read her mind. I don't want to get in the middle of things. She's pissed that you went, that's all I know. Maybe give her a few days to calm down?"

Her smile came into my memory, when we held each other and stared into each other's eyes until we would both start laughing, knowing how lucky we were to have one another. That warm fuzzy feeling flooding me as I felt I would melt into her. I ought to find her now, to apologise and get Nathaniel out of my flat and stand by my lover. Gulping, isolation overcame my heart knowing I was too late. On the shelf by the tv, the photo of us taken on holiday a few years ago. When we were human, when we were in love.

My heart fell into my boots, why did I always mess up? As a mortal I was never this inconsistent. Sometimes I really hated being a vampire.

"I had an awful dream that something happened to her. I want to see her. Are you sure you don't know anything else? Please don't say you don't to protect me, I'm already angry at myself."

"She's fine; I'll keep an eye on things. Don't worry so much." He returned to his book, but my anger welled up. It was easy for him to say that, sitting there in her home reading. That should be me, and if we hadn't of met him...

"Anthony, if you hadn't of met me, Nathaniel would've still showed up at your place." Completely unfazed by my erratic thoughts he got up, walked over and put a hand on my shoulder.

"Look, I've had my share of lovers," shaking his head he sighed. "Human women can be...tricky. Especially if you're an immortal. Their jealousy, insecurity," grunting he continued, "God knows how much harder if you're a vampire. But supernatural women, men, that's a whole new level of..." he stopped here considering his words carefully, "*Complexity*. Her emotions run high- as do yours. Just chill the fuck out, you've got a lifetime to argue with each other." Smiling he turned and fell back onto the sofa.

I decided to head off to the studio and turn my anxiety into creativity. Before I was a vampire, this is what I did. I used art to express what I couldn't face emotionally. It was better than having all my feelings bottled up.

I wanted to create a sculpture that was an abstract mythological beast—half man, half bird. I worked furiously like never before. Within twelve hours I made the kind of progress that would have taken weeks, maybe months when I was human. I was relentless. I melded metal, soldering the structure together, cooling it, fusing it. After some hours my hair and face were damp with sweat and dirt. But my mind felt rested and my soul felt alive again.

The sculpture was twisted and beautiful, its face calling to me and its body, sublime and dark. Poised as if to spring forward, the creature was made from metal strips, obscure and tormented. I stood back in wonder. It depicted something from within both beautiful and terrible; the heart of this vampire.

I sat down in front of it to immerse myself in its presence, its essence, wiping the sweat from my face onto my sleeves. I couldn't take a picture of it. That would seem too demeaning to its abominable power. I was astonished at my ability. When I'd been human, I always dreamed of being a great artist, but I also always failed at making the grade. I finished the sculpture and felt a strong compulsion to see Rachel. I'd vented my emotions for now so I could see my lover again.

Feeling alive and refreshed I headed back to Rachel and Marcus. I passed a few vampires on my way back, they kept their distance from me. What they had heard about me, whether about Emidius or taking down the Elite, I didn't know which, but I wasn't keen on interacting with most vampires.

I had noticed that there were fewer vampires after the war. I supposed many had fled or been killed, but either way it was better for the humans.

Thinking about getting back to Rachel's home promoted me to think about Nathaniel. I would have to try and keep his name out of mind with Marcus prying into my thoughts

It was quiet in the house when I let myself in and I noticed Marcus wasn't about. I crept up the stairs and opened the door to Rachel's bedroom to find her fast asleep. I stood there watching her and then slipped in beside her, wrapping myself around her cool body.

Sleep fell upon me fast and dreams of disturbing and sinister creatures enveloped my sub-consciousness. I dreamt of a man, young and covered with tattoos including some on his face but strikingly handsome. He stood over me with my life in his young hands, laughing and speaking in a language that I didn't recognise. His long black hair flowed gently behind him as if he was caught in a breeze and the way he looked at Rachel repulsed me.

An awful power emanated from him. He seemed a malevolent creature.

Shadows encased me and I felt confined, claustrophobic and smothered by dark figures, similar to the attack that made me what I am. Deep and ethereal voices echoed around where ever I was.

But these dark figures were different and reminded me of Marcus.

I was vaguely aware of thrashing and turning in my sleep and awoke some hours later, my dead heart pumping furiously. Looking at Rachel she was peaceful and slept like the dead. I had to get up, I couldn't sleep, adrenalin coursing through me. It was only five-thirty am. I went to find Marcus, but still he wasn't there.

Steadying myself in the shower my eyes wanted to close, and my nerves seemed shot. I went to wake Rachel. My instinct told me that danger was upon us.

Marcus made me jump. He came bounding up the stairs, his expression one of shock, his eyes wide.

"I know," I said quietly. "Are they here now?"

He nodded and looked at my lover who was so oblivious to the danger.

"Get them away from here. You promised," I said as calmly as I could muster.

His face a mix of concern and defeat, he turned and fled back down the stairs.

"Rachel, Rachel, get up. We've got to go!" I spoke urgently shaking her.

She mumbled and made no effort to move so I had to step up my efforts. I had to speak quietly. "Get up, we're in danger." I threw some clothes at her and she sat up quickly looking confused. I put my finger to my lips to keep her from talking loudly, hoping our presence could go undetected for as long as possible.

She looked at me in shock, whether for waking her or due to our situation, probably both. I used the opportunity to text Nathaniel. Hopefully he could help or bring help if needed. Sent. In a minute she was dressed and her face was stern with determination. Both of us breathing steadily, we crept towards the back bedroom window.

I could hear Marcus talking to others downstairs and felt the cold air through the open front door. So far so good.

Life though! When you're trying to be quiet you seem to make more noise. The window was old and opening without force impossible.

Neither of us spoke and our footsteps were light, but we couldn't control the squeak and groan of the window opening.

We held our breath, hoping no one heard us open it. When we heard nothing change, I poked my head out the window.

And below they waited for us. Marcus's kin. The nephilim.

There was no point in trying to run now. Even if we could succeed in out-running them, which would be hard, we would have to stay running indefinitely.

Looking out I saw a woman in a brown leather bomber jacket, cargo pants and boots, weapons strapped about her, stood below watching me. Her short black hair highlighted her stern beauty. Next to her, a guy with bright red hair and mirrored glasses grinned up, looking expectantly at us to make a run for it. Unlike the boy from my dream, I didn't feel an evil presence from them, but I didn't feel a kind one either.

We turned around, shut the window, and tentatively went downstairs to find Marcus.

He was talking to a young man with fine blonde hair, dark eyebrows and full lips that gave him the look of a cherub. His eyes though betrayed his youthful looks, deep and sorrowful. His eyes, like Marcus's, were completely grey, though not as dark and he looked at us in wonder.

"Anthony, may I introduce Acacius." Marcus spoke calmly.

"Hello. I have been looking forward to meeting you." He walked towards me and reached out to shake my hand. The nephilim, so formal and polite, his voice preternaturally deep like Marcus's and seemed to echo throughout the room.

I reached out to shake his hand without thought, although the confusion and hesitation I felt probably showed on my face.

"Um, hello. Why are you here? What do you mean, 'looking forward to meeting' me?"

"News of Marcus's deeds has reached far. He is the first of his kind to take the blood of a vampire. We are simply the first to arrive." And here he paused. "I have known Marcus for a long time. He always was mischievous." He smiled. "And we've known about you, too. A vampire saved by a demi-god is a rare thing indeed. Quite unheard of actually. We mean you no harm. You are right to be fearful. Had you been any other vampire we would kill you on sight, but as I said with the blood of Emidius you must be unique."

I couldn't help but let out a sigh of relief. *Thank you, Emidius.* It was just as well I had been infected by that demon before. Otherwise, I wouldn't have been saved by her.

Acacius chuckled and answered my thoughts, "It wasn't a demon that attacked you, it was the Experimentals created by Tyrell."

"I know. I know only too well. We tried to destroy them, but they were too strong. I hope Emidius succeeded where we failed."

Acacius smiled grimly, but didn't answer and I wondered then if perhaps Emidius had left the Experimentals to the hands of the nephilim. I had no idea where that thought came from.

Behind Marcus and Acacius the other two entered and Acacius introduced them to us. "This is Halina and Aaron."

She nodded, her expression unchanged from before but Aaron with his wild red hair smiled even more widely. "So, I smell Lucius has been here? After you no-doubt." Aaron glanced at Rachel as he spoke.

Lucius? Who the hell is Lucius? He's been here? After my Rachel and I hadn't noticed? Why Rachel? All these thoughts flew through my mind, one after another stirring my anger, disbelief, fear, and confusion.

Before I could answer, Halina replied, her voice stark, "A demon!"

I looked at Marcus for an explanation. He replied, "I know he has some vampire friends. I assumed you knew about demons."

At which point Halina snorted.

"What do you mean, after me?" Rachel barked. "What the Hell?"

Aaron smiled again, amused and glancing from me to Rachel asked, "Are you two together?" I shot him a look and he added quickly, "I only ask because Lucius has one intention only. To breed. Like most demons, or as they're called in legend, Incubi, they want to have the most powerful offspring. So they spend their existence screwing every female they can in the hopes some of these children will be powerful. Not very original I know, and you would think he'd need something else to occupy his time. But I guess not."

As Aaron finished speaking I stared in bewilderment at Rachel, who stood open mouthed in an expression of shock and horror.

Realizing how cavalier he sounded, Aaron's perpetual grin dropped and he winked at me and Rachel sheepishly. "Sorry. I know I sound harsh and possibly too cheerful. I just say what I observe. I mean no harm."

Anger welled up inside me that some demon had intruded Rachel's home. When I glanced at her, her face appeared stern. I put my hand on her arm reassuringly.

Marcus responded to me. "Calm yourself. You do not know what you are dealing with. Demons can be very formidable, even for you." Then turning to Aaron, "Enough, Aaron! You really should think before you speak to other immortals. Look, I've never heard of a demon wanting to be with a vampire, they always choose human mates, so I didn't think you'd have anything to fear. If I thought you did, I would've said. Demons are unstable and flighty creatures and don't usually concern themselves with other paranormals."

"Come, we need to talk." Acacius was gracious in his manner. "Others are aware of what you have done and where you are, Marcus. They are not happy and demand your blood in the name of justice. And Anthony, many know how Emidius saved your life. And now Marcus has sought you out, they are coming. Some are angry, some are already unruly and will look to taste your blood."

My worst fears confirmed. For the next few moments I went into complete denial, into my private escape of being mortal again. Being mortal with Rachel, living carefree with worries so minor compared to this supernatural existence.

Marcus spoke abruptly. "Anthony! Listen to Acacius! He has your best interests at heart."

Acacius continued, "Are you really so surprised?" He spoke softly. "I mean how many vampires do you think have the blood of a demi-god in their veins? I'm surprised you hadn't been sought out earlier. At least with us here, we can help you and Rachel."

"If all of you"—and I looked at Marcus—"if you weren't here we wouldn't have this to worry about! But what of the demon; why now?" I didn't know how, but I knew that his undoing had spelled disaster for us all. I also wasn't naive enough to realise that their protection was for nothing, and felt sure just as the others were making their way to me now, these nephilim wanted to taste my blood.

"Of course we do," Marcus said quietly. "I for one could smell the bitter sweetness of your blood the first time we met. Even Rachel has a hint of it. You're stronger than most now. I'm sure you were told this."

"We will not kill you or her." Halina spoke with cool authority. "Some nephilim, taking Marcus's insane example, will look to drink the blood of vampires. I feel it. They know of you and your woman, but I doubt in the first instance they will hunt you. Most will revere you, afraid of your power. Of course, had Marcus not broken every rule we have ever had, none of this would've befallen you."

Acacius moved in front of me and put a reassuring hand on my arm. "I do not wish to drink your blood." And looking at Rachel, he continued, "Or any vampires blood for that matter. Curiosity doesn't have that much of a hold on me." He smiled and I felt a genuine warmth from him. But trust, that would still be foolish.

Running my hands over my face, I sighed and asked the question I didn't really want an answer to. "Demons, nephilim...is there anything else I should know about?"

"Yes." Marcus moved alongside Acacius and leaned earnestly towards me. "You felt them. I heard and felt this from your thoughts, when you picked up Rachel after she had burned Nathaniel. They were in the tree line. You remember?"

I felt the urge to sit down as all this information was pouring out. All my dreams of living quietly in the shadows with

Rachel, hunting evil-doers by night and spending our free time pursuing our passions. It was slipping away fast like water from a hand. I slumped on the sofa before I asked, not really knowing if I wanted the answer. "What *was* that?" As the words fell from my mouth, I shuddered remembering the cold fear I had felt every day since when I thought about it.

Cluttered in Rachel's tiny living room, I'd thought Marcus took up a lot of space, but with four of them as well it was like being squeezed into a tin can. Nephilim are taller than most humans, including Halina. She was the shortest at six foot, the men around six-five or six-seven for Aaron and Marcus.

Rachel and I sat on the arms of the chair allowing our *guests* the sofa and the chair, the atmosphere was more relaxed than I would have thought possible, though Rachel and I were still not one-hundred percent trusting. These creatures effused a sense of quiet power and serenity.

Marcus looked at Acacius, his expression stern. "Werewolves. You saw werewolves."

I laughed abruptly. I couldn't help it, it just flew out. "You have to be kidding, right? I must be in a horror movie or something. Rachel, we need to make a list; vampires, werewolves, demons and nephilim! Go on; what else? Hang on, where's the garlic, where's the silver!"

"You forgot Emidius!" Acacius laughed. "She might not forgive you of that!" He continued, "Spirits, banshees. Monsters of the psyche made manifest by the power of the human mind. But alongside our fears of what lays in wait in the shadows, there is also good. Everything has opposites—wealth verses poverty, health verses illness, good versus evil. Where you stand right now determines what you attract in."

Acacius smiled and sat back, studying me with a fascination. I guess under normal circumstances he'd kill me in an instant. But these were not normal times.

"How can I be sure you won't kill me?" I asked the others.

"Because..." Aaron stood up and walked over as he spoke. "Because we are going to give you something no other vampire has ever managed to attain. We are going to allow you to drink from us!" Aaron stood up, full of wide-eyed eagerness.

I couldn't help but raise my eyebrows and laugh. "Nice try, but your blood is lethal to me!"

His words tripping over his tongue, Aaron was animated, gesturing wildly. "Probably not. Not with *her* blood in you. We think you could...benefit from our blood."

"Why would you care?" Now I was suspicious. "I am not interested in being bound to another being. What if I don't care for your blood? And most importantly why would you give me something so Divine? I have, after all, a power now that is unmatched by most vampires, as you've just said. What do you hope to gain by giving me your blood?"

It was Marcus's turn to laugh raucously now, leaning forward, his enthusiasm pouring out. "They have both thought about it- about drinking my blood. Come, should we go upstairs now?"

"What if you're wrong? What if I die horribly burning from the inside out, as you said?"

"Come, Anthony, second guessing, that's not like you."

"And I note that none of you have answered Anthony's question. Why? What's in it for you?" Rachel got up, looking them in the eyes.

"There is no one reason." Halina's voice commanded attention when she spoke. "*They* are coming, the veil has torn and you can help *more* with our blood to boost your own. We will need your help."

"What now? You want to do this now?" I shrieked.

"Yes, before the others arrive and chaos follows them," Aaron added urgently.

"And you want to taste the blood of a vampire? You hate vampires."

"Her blood runs through your veins. For that, for a taste we would do anything, pay any price," Acacius answered on behalf of the others.

"Except you? You don't want to though?"

"I admit, I am intrigued but no. I do not, but I am not as the other nephilim. Let's just say I lead a higher existence."

Aaron went to speak but Acacius shot him a look so he shut up.

"What does that mean, higher existence?" I could see he was agitated by my questions, but I had to ask since mine and Rachel's lives were on the line.

"It means, Anthony, I do not partake in many things that other nephilim involve themselves in. I hunt, I write, I pray. That is what I do."

I could see by his body language that was the end of that discussion and I thought it wise not to think about it, seeing as he'd read my thoughts.

He smiled in acknowledgement of that last thought.

Marcus knelt before me as I extended my wrist and in that moment the atmosphere changed to exalted expectation. My face grew hot, and looking at the floor to avoid eye contact as the place went deathly quiet, all eyes were on us. Swallowing hard, my mouth dry, I tentatively offered him my wrist.

He bit my wrist, it was so easy for him now he was part vampire. The others gasped. What they were watching, they had never witnessed before.

The abject horror, a nephilim kneeling to a vampire and drinking *his* blood. My blood. A tremor of sensation shot up me—excitement, taboo—when Marcus's teeth broke my skin and hot, searing desire enwrapped me. I was in heaven, ironically with this fallen angel at my feet. Moaning as he drank I felt the power of his passion surge out of him as I sat there wrapped up in this experience with him.

Mustering all my strength to pull my wrist away, I expected him to fall to the floor, but instead he looked at me with his strange dark eyes, now seemingly glimmering a lighter grey-almost silver as he moved his shaggy dark hair aside. Before I realised what I was doing, I was sitting next to him, locked onto his neck like a vice. I ran my tongue over his skin. His scent was warm and dark and I inhaled him before I bit. He shuddered and I pulled him into me as I drank that divine blood. Like electricity coursing through me and filling every part of my body. Drunk on his blood, my tongue was numb and tingled as the hot liquid passed through my mouth and then warm down my throat and stomach, like wine. I couldn't let go, couldn't stop, and I was connected with his thoughts as the fiery blood buzzed and quivered in my body.

Like I was dreaming. His heart pounded fast, then slowed, I was swept away in his thoughts, his emotions. Was this real? My body swayed and his heat seeped into me, I didn't care whether this was reality or not. I just wanted his warmth, his blood, hot and fierce.

In my mind I saw an island, warm and rustic, the splashing of the tide on the rocks, and I believed in that moment that nothing I had lived was real. Would I wake up from this fascinating dream?

His blood was a drug. I wanted more, but at some point he pushed me away and I became vaguely aware that I was lying on the floor, suddenly cold and alone without him, staring up at the ceiling at flashes and orbs of lights. Seeing sounds move across like fireflies with my head rolling like a ship in a storm. I heard voices come from his mind and saw pictures moving across my mind of him in a desert.

I remember seeing, in my mind's eye, fear as I watched a strange vision of a young boy in a medieval village with vampires, contorted and twisted faces like something from a painting. They were tormenting him. I was the boy and I knew they were sent to kill me. Then a huge presence behind me, blinding them, and then stillness. Coming back into the present, I looked around the room and saw many wraith-like spirits drifting around Aaron and Halina. But Acacius, Acacius in this state looked like a blaze of white light. Ghostly, priest-like figures surrounded him and stood at a distance in prayer as in great reverence. I remember Acacius smiling at me and saying something but what I don't recall now.

Both of us were intoxicated. I saw Marcus's shape as he sat against the sofa in a state of wonder. Hours passed and my awareness of my surroundings started to sharpen again.

When I came around, the others were sitting and talking earnestly while music played. I remember my body thrumming to the sound of pounding beats that took my mind to another landscape. Lethargy washed over me and it took me some time to push myself up.

The experience was too strong for words. Both Marcus and I were silent for many hours and the others were aware enough not to press this.

Rachel had abstained from tasting the nephilim for the time being, wanting to see what effect I had from Marcus.

I left early evening. I needed to get away, my head still reeling. I needed to walk, to clear my mind and get some air. I didn't want to go back to them there so I headed off towards the city.

Your Cold Vampire Heart

Rachel

ANTHONY LEFT WITH MARCUS'S blood in his veins whilst Acacius, Aaron, and Halina left to go back to their rented home. Marcus stayed with me, but I wanted time alone. Walking upstairs I flung myself on my bed, my mind frenzied with questions and my heart telling me something was wrong.

With Anthony's reckless behaviour in the past and fuelled with the blood of that fallen angel, his emotions would be on fire. I wished he had chosen to share that with me. I knew where he was going. It was instinct for him—straight to Nathaniel.

Although Anthony hadn't mentioned anything to me, my instinct told me that Nathaniel, my maker, was alive. Although Nathaniel had scared and threatened me, that bond, that pull was stronger than the threat itself.

And I understand why Anthony would be drawn to Nathaniel, aside from their deep bond. During the war, Anthony had been mutilated by one of the Elite and it was Nathaniel who saved him. Not by blood, but by splicing his own genes into Anthony.

Deep in my heart, though it nauseated me to admit it, the bond we once had as humans would never return to us as vampires.

It was time to make a choice. If I stayed with Anthony I would always be second in his life, second to Nathaniel, and although Anthony would not willingly choose that, the fact remained that having such a physical connection with Nathaniel, it could not be altered.

Numbness consumed my heart, my body tight, holding in emotion. I knew this wasn't the future I'd chosen, being second to another.

Cutting ties to both *was* the only choice, but it was heart wrenching. I would have to tell Anthony when he eventually came back, but for now I would console myself in the company of Marcus.

Despondency overwhelmed me and the knowledge of immortality made the situation heavier. Potentially I could carry this feeling for decades, even centuries.

Marcus sensed my mood and tentatively asked if he could accompany me as I headed out. I just shrugged. I didn't care. He went to speak and I knew in that moment he had read my mind and was about to advise me on Anthony, and I swear to God it was the best thing that he shut up.

From that point on he kept quiet and followed me. I needed a thrill, something to lift my depleted spirits, along with blood. I think I was having an existential crisis. I mean, all I do is feast on blood. It drives me to distraction and any semblance of normality seems to seep from my life faster than water from hands. I had to at least try and control myself, my emotions, my cravings.

I arrived at a bar, and things grew more heated. The deep pounding of the music coupled with the mass of hot mortal bodies, sweaty and bursting made Marcus look like he was ready for dinner.

His face lit up and he beamed a smile. We spotted a lot of other vampires in there, mixing easily with the humans, laughing, touching, thrashing around to the heavy music. It felt like my lucky night. I watched as Marcus made his way to the bar and I decided to hang back, knowing that as a vampire it wouldn't be long before they came to me. The mortal males, so young, offered to buy me a drink. Of course I obliged and whilst one of them went off to the bar his friend asked me questions. I had to listen but in my mind I thought, I could turn him and take him with me for eternity.

Marcus boisterously made his way through the crowd, smiling and carrying his drink and a drink for me which he instinctively put on a table next to me knowing I could never touch it. I introduced the man I was talking to, his face betrayed his feelings of inadequacy against Marcus. I told him Marcus was my cousin. Ah, relief for him.

Then Marcus wandered off to mix with the other immortals, some of whom were watching us, while the others wildly threw themselves around in the crowd to the fast pounding beats. They were working themselves into a frenzy and watching them made me feel untamed. I forgot my troubles with temptation surrounding me. Anthony was with Nathaniel. Life was never going to be as it was before. We had slept in the dark crypt together for three months after the war with Tyrell, in hiding. Now I had to move on.

Impulsively I grabbed at the man—I didn't hear his name—and kissed him. His lips were soft and warm against my cold lips. As I pulled him into me, I felt a pity then. He couldn't fight back or resist. Was it fair? I couldn't help myself though, he was vital, full of life and passion. I was angry and empty and needed a fix. But he held no evil intent and guilt. I couldn't harm one so innocent, could I?

A vampire approached us and pulled us apart, smiling.

"I'm Damien. You're Rachel? You should leave him alone; he's always here. He knows what you are and he's as addicted to your blood as you are to his. Wouldn't you rather be with an equal?" He winked, still smiling, which made me laugh. Before I could answer Damien pulled me gently into his arms, his cool body next to mine.

I sighed. "Yes, I want an equal." Damien was really tall, his black hair fell over half of his face, and he dressed like someone from two decades ago. Leather, black and erotic. His white skin clashed beautifully with his hair, but his kiss, slow and meandering, sent a shudder of expectation through me. He kissed like a gentleman and I could stay there, locked with him forever. I forgot everything. We were like two teenagers kissing and stopping only to look into each other's eyes.

"You should come with me," he breathed at last.

"Why should I do that?"

"You know why. You're nephilim friend, you need to get away from him. He spells death to you, and your lover, everyone knows about him having her blood in him and his bond with Nathaniel. Come with me, we could leave this place. I don't live far."

It was tempting, I wanted him and he was one hundred percent right about Anthony. Before I could say more Marcus came over looking concerned with a girl clinging to his arm, but he acted as if he didn't notice. "Rachel! You're leaving, so soon?" Looking at Damien who avoided eye contact he continued, "I understand, I know. We can meet up later, just shout."

So I left with Damien, his presence was soothing to my soul. As we walked through the busy streets, his flat was right in the centre over-looking a small park.

In his flat, everything was black, various animal skulls adorned the walls and large dark paintings of emotional torment . The only lighting, red and blue low lights and the sweet musky incense produced thick wisps of smoke. Sublime Gothic music played softly, so fitting with the few candles flickering. He'd set his scene, an art of seduction he'd practised for how long? The atmosphere was enticingly Byronic. Taking off his jacket, he welcomed me to his huge sofa as he sat there.

He was so alluring, I was completely drawn to him but I wanted to get to know this man first. So I sat at the other end of the sofa.

"Your place is very...retro. And dark..."

He laughed. "Yes, I guess it is. I hadn't noticed really. God, I've only lived here just over ten years. To think, I could have the same decor for a century and never notice! What an awful thought..." he chuckled.

"It's good to meet another with the same problems, you're right. Eternity seems incomprehensible and daunting. And full of problems I'd never have imagined." I got up and looked across the square. "I could stand here in a hundred years, in two hundred years and the buildings, the green would look the same way they did when they were built three hundred years ago, but the people would look and dress differently. Life would be different, but we would remain the same. That's depressing." My existential crisis was not over yet.

"I am truly sorry," Damien said, getting up and walking over. "It's these walls, isn't it? The dark foreboding eighties Goth look? I promise, I'll paint them white tomorrow and it can look twenty-first century!"

His grin and raised eyebrows made me smile. I knew he was trying to lighten the mood, and in a way, yes, I'd have to keep up if I wanted to survive. But that was kind of the point. I didn't want to survive, I wanted to live. To know that you will die, it somehow puts more urgency on life, you only have a finite time. You work to fulfil your dreams, but to live forever, endlessly craving the blood of humans, that incredible high, that alone feels like existence. Not living.

He moved tentatively closer, and gently put his arms around me as we gazed out of the window.

"I haven't been like this for a century, but it would be something to stand here in a hundred years with you," he whispered.

Looking up at his face, into his eyes I held him tighter. His lips touched mine, so delicately, but I knew I had to close one door before opening another.

"I have to go, but I will be back," he dropped his arms, neither of us said anything and I made my way home to finish that chapter of my life.

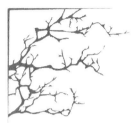

Firedrake

Marcus

AS RACHEL WENT WITH Damien, I was left for the first time to explore this city with other vampires.

Their behaviour was bold compared with my friends. We headed towards the other side of the city and piled into a night club, it was heaving with mortals. Neon lights flashed, music thumping and bodies packed tightly, dancing, sweaty in the tiny club.

Torin, the vampire male who'd invited me squeezed his way through the people, reaching the other side I saw him staring at a woman- a human who subserviently got up from her chair and walked over to him- almost in a trance.

Pushing her against the wall, he turned his back on the crowd as he bent over her neck, her eyes flickered and her face stupefied. Sweat broke over me as I watched, he being so brazen in public.

Looking for the others I'd come in with, they, too, were involved with women, pushed their victims against the sticky black walls and drank from their victims. No mortal seemed to notice, as I scanned the room I noticed a man watching me, as my eyes met his he glanced away and moved fast across the club. He wasn't human, he was a shifter, a lycan or some kind.

He darted out the door so quickly even I had a job to catch up to him, pushing my way through the crowd, human hands grabbed and groped at me, I was taken aback.

Outside I couldn't see him, but I picked up his scent, for a few seconds my legs swayed as my body buzzed with sensations from those women's touches. My body wanted to go back in but my mind was more intrigued with the creature that had bolted out.

There was something different about the way he moved. I'd come across lycans many times and the way they moved, walked, or ran was certainly more animalistic, seeming to use the whole of their body, their torsos almost lunging forwards unlike humans or vampires whose movement is mainly in the legs. But this one was unusual.

Running away from the club, I spied him in the distance, as he ran he not only lunged slightly forward with his body, his legs and feet sprung from the floor with each step, his arms and shoulders automatically bobbing back and forth with his legs. I wondered if he would take off at any moment. Keeping my distance, I didn't want him to know I was following him. He ran up through the outskirts of the city and into the park, stopping abruptly to catch his breath.

Shadows from the trees emerged, their smell filling my senses, earthy and musky. I knew what these creatures were by their scent alone. Lycans. Powerful, wild, and almost impossible to kill, especially in a pack.

Instinctively I gulped and stayed completely still, trying my hardest to quiet my breathing. Moving only my eyes, I hoped they wouldn't smell me. But I could fly off, if I was fast enough.

The man collapsed to his knees, his hands reaching to the ground to stop himself falling flat upon the ground as one of the lycans strode forward, his limbs moving like clouds, fast and soft.

"Luke? What happened?" The huge man whispered. Others edged a little further from the tree line, all in their human form. They were right to stay out of the city, God only knew if my blood-filled kin drank from them, what would happen.

But this Luke couldn't speak, gasping he clawed at the earth beneath him, the alpha man stretching out his arms to back the others off, stepping back from Luke.

A sound of cracking as Luke yelled out, his head bent forward, face crimson with rage and pain and that chilling sound of snapping bones. Groaning in agony, his knuckles white with pain I watched as his shirt burst open on his back, revealing sharp curved ridges bursting slowly through his skin, blood oozing around them. Gripping the tree, my vision blurred as I clung tighter, swooning in shock- I had never seen a transformation in all my years. Pain in my fingers, raw and deep as I realised I was grabbing at the bark with all my strength, my body tense like an over-wound toy. Slowly I released my breath, feeling my heart slow a little as I spied this creature undergoing his shift.

The alpha spoke softly to this Luke, but he couldn't hear anything I guessed. Wails of agony, searing pain as his flesh ripped, torn, a reptilian creature emerging. His face split, more blood seeped out and my senses sent me into a torment of crav-ing.

A tail emerged, bursting, ripping through the end of his back, and in the next few seconds everything sped up, hands, limbs, torn and stretched. In front of me was a dragon.

My legs straining, fighting my urge to watch as my instinct was driving me to run, it took all my wits to contain myself, my wings, my body from flight. That wouldn't save me now This dragon, long, twisted, snake like, its scales the size of my hands and its reptile eyes, its snout lifted, nostrils sniffing as he stretched out his massive leathery wings. A gust of wind blew past me from the beating of its mighty wings. Holy shit, I didn't even know such creatures existed. And this one only a few feet away from me could eat me like a light snack, and had joined with lycans. Peering, I saw the alpha man had no fear of this dragon, the creature glancing at him, then its great head faced forward away from him as it bellowed out fire, scorching the grass in front of it.

It shook its smoky head, looked at the alpha who nodded slightly, and swiftly started running, then took off with a speed that was shocking compared to his size. I fell behind the tree, allowing my tensed muscles to collapse and I slouched on the ground against the tree, sweat pouring from my forehead. I could hear him circling above, Luke, flying too high to be spot-ted by my kin or any other paranormal. I needed to speak to him, to these shifters. They could help stop the atrocity of demons and wraiths. But right now, I had had enough.

Burning

Rachel

ANTHONY WAITED FOR me upstairs, laying on the bed, presuming. It was now or never. My stomach turned, and heart flipped. I loved him but he was bad for me. Before he could speak, I did...

"You know I always thought we'd be together forever. After you were bitten, I knew something chilling had happened to you, I knew you were infected. And you were. Not just with vampire blood, but with lies. And I know I slept with Nathaniel way back, but he was, he *is* my maker and my will was under his influence. You had no such excuse and I now realize that I can never trust you. I love you, but I won't trust you.

"But you, you never really came back to me. I hoped with all my heart back in that crypt, that we could start again. But you were never really with me, not then, not before, and definitely not now. And now you're seeing Nathaniel and you think that I didn't know that. I am numb now, I'm done. You and the nephilim need to leave. I don't want to talk about it, and I'm not arguing about it. I need time alone."

His face dropped, and it took all my strength not to back down. His eyes teared and his body slumped down on the bed. He was dumbstruck. I know it was a shock to him, but I couldn't stay with him knowing he would always, in the end, put Nathaniel before me. I wondered then if Nathaniel had known this all along. By becoming my maker and saving Anthony, he had beholden both of us to him. My mouth was dry and my stomach felt empty and sick as the pain of letting him go overwhelmed me. But I had to.

"I admit I was with Nathaniel," Anthony blurted out, pale with shock.

"He's very clever. When Alexander took you, Nathaniel had some of his genes from the infection- his bacterial strain of this disease, injected into you. We *are* bound by blood, but by the infected organism, more so. He could've just given you his blood. Now you are part of him like no-other except like me, who he turned. He has ensured that everyone is dependent upon him. And don't worry, I know you won't agree with me, after all I am not him. But you and he can have a lifetime debating that. I know you were with him. I don't want to be with you any longer. If you had chosen me over him...but you never will. The saddest thing is, I could do the same, I have more connection with him, but I chose to be stronger and break that. You didn't, you won't. You chose him. Just leave."

With that, I grabbed up some of his clothes and handed them to him. Anger was ready to burst out of me, but I held on.

He just sat there, mute with his mouth open. I had to turn away. I couldn't face a life time of this, of being second best to my lover. No one needs that.

"Rachel, I know I've been scattered. I am sorry, truly. I am not ready to throw us away, please."

"I *can't* do this. If you were sincere you would've told me about Nathaniel. You didn't, you kept that a secret and so I have to wonder, what else aren't you telling me? No, don't answer that, I don't want to know. It's finished, enough already. Just go now. I'm going out, be gone by the time I get back."

I grabbed my coat and left.

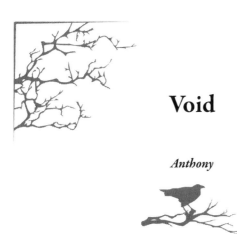

Void

Anthony

AS I WALKED DOWNSTAIRS and into her living room, Marcus answered the question that burned in my mind and my stomach, "No, I haven't slept with her." He said it so casually as his massive form slouched on the tiny couch. He didn't even look up from his book.

"Has she met someone else?" I was shocked as this thought came into my head and tumbled straight out of my mouth. A moment ago I hadn't even conceived of the idea.

"Why do you want to know? You know she's right, I know she's right."

Striding over I grabbed that bloody book from his hands and flung it across the room. "Let me enlighten you, divine one! You're in *my* place. If you were not *still* here, I wouldn't have had to leave to get some peace. You've become a burden, why don't you let me drink you dry now and rid you of your self-inflicted suffering?"

I smirked as I saw the affect my words on his face as his jaw dropped.

"After all, let me remind you that it was you that brought this upon yourself! You said you drank the blood of a vampire because you were bored! *I* never had a choice, I was attacked by vicious blood suckers, whilst you wallow around reading. Your sense of entitlement sickens me. You expect everyone else to clean up your mistake. We helped you, remember? And you promised not to stay long and yet...you're still here," I yelled.

Marcus, the epitome of kindness watched me as I vented my anger, throwing my mistakes onto him. Don't get me wrong, I meant some of it, but really I knew I had brought this on myself. And I didn't want to admit it. I was being asked to leave, and he wasn't. That made me sick.

After a few moments of silence, he walked over to me. My head was bowed in shame and I covered my eyes to hide the tears. Putting a hand on my shoulder, he spoke quietly.

"That dark power changes most, if not all. Thoughts that have laid hidden rise to the surface and once released cannot be pushed away. I think probably you are not the settling down type. You are more like Nathaniel than you care to imagine. He loved once, a long time ago. But after his lover died he was never the same. After you were turned you raged out of control, and in that time something awakened in you, something that will not lie dormant. So you separate. Eternity is a long time. Maybe in the future...who knows? C'mon, we don't have much stuff here. I'll sort out getting a place or staying with Acacius. I know you, Anthony, better than yourself."

Reluctantly, I gathered my clothes and few belongings. I also carefully guarded my thoughts. Nathaniel though...I never knew.

Marcus gathered up his few possessions and without another word we walked slowly across the city to my flat. Nausea
gripped my stomach and I felt hollow thinking that I would
spend eternity alone. Being with her before I was turned was
comforting, almost like we had shared a past life together and
I had a companion to be with in this new existence. All who I
met now, I would never have that bond with. I really would be
cutting myself away from my past human life.

"Anthony, calm your thoughts, this is just one instance of
pain. If you're going to live for eternity, you'll need to toughen
up. Trust me, I've lived centuries, and friends come and some
go. Who knows, in a few decades or a century you two could
be together again, stronger than ever. I know right now that
doesn't seem a comfort, but for immortals time passes quickly.
And maybe then you'll have both found yourselves. You're too
young a vampire to comprehend this now."

"I underestimated you." I felt some relief that I had this
wise, crazy soul as a friend.

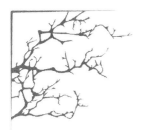

Damien

Rachel

MY HEART SANK AS I left my home to see Damien, seeking comfort in his company. Despondent and heavy, I trudged across the city, my throat dry and scratchy.

His company felt serene. More soul and less ego, if that's possible for a vampire.

He seemed to understand how complex and deadly our existence is rather than the ongoing lust for blood. I loved this city and as a mortal could easily think of living there for all my days, but as an immortal it was too small. It couldn't contain me, but I didn't know yet where I wanted to go.

Damien answered his door as if he'd been expecting me and welcomed me in like an old friend. It was a relief. I didn't want to hunt tonight. I just wanted to talk, to muse, to act like a human.

His flat was smoky with incense and he had candles burning as before, music on quietly, and a book that he was reading on his sofa. Amongst the incense, there was a musty scent in the air and it brought back the nostalgia of my first flat, a smell so familiar and comforting. I hadn't noticed before that his flat was so full of antiques and antiquities. Amongst the candles sat curios dating back to Victorian times—old clocks, trinkets, and tiny mirrors. Then tiny Egyptian sculptures that looked real—Bast, Thoth, Horus—and beside them, pagan deities. All packed in the mantel piece and shelves amongst piles and piles of old leather bound books.

"Is that wine?"

His face reddened. "Yes. I know I can't drink it but I like to pretend! One of my quirks. And this is Victor, my cat."

"Hello, Victor." I bent to stroke his head, his long ginger and white fur like velvet to touch. "He's beautiful. I didn't meet him last time."

"Well, Victor has his own life, too. I have a garden out the back; he's often there exploring. So, have you gotten over your existential crisis? Or is the thought of immortality still too much to bear?" he asked, grinning and winking at me. It was so easy with him, we were like kindred spirits and his laid-back playfulness was refreshing. No drama. "I ask because every immortal goes through this, some earlier than others. And for every vampire I ever met, at the beginning everything seems out of control, rushed, one disaster to the next." As he finished talking he sank into the sofa, smelling the fine red wine.

"I'm thinking of leaving Bath."

"Of course you are. It's so small, too many immortals. I was turned abroad so I had the unfortunate problem of learning how to exist, or rather I had to learn to exist in a place I neither knew nor spoke the language. But I empathise with you. It's all perfectly natural."

He sat there, so calm, the complete opposite of Anthony. He, reassuring and gentle, the candlelight casting flickering shadows across his face. Victor jumped up and settled on his lap as Damien held his wine in one hand, the other instinctively stroking his elderly cat. Victor didn't seem an ordinary cat to me, but I said nothing.

"Then how are you so calm? How have you come to terms with the insatiable lust for blood driving you, being thrown into one supernatural disaster to the next?"

"Ah! The blood thing. I don't know whether it lessens with time or whether you just get used to it. I learned to keep a low profile, to avoid detection by other species. I exist almost as a human...almost. I rarely think about immortality. I can't because it seems too impossible. But I get lonely. But so do humans. I do enjoy fine wine though!" he laughed.

"Could you teach me? I want to be invisible to the others." Relief flooded through me and the despondent state started to lift, being here with him. Here was a man who had managed to find calm in an existence that defied rational thought. I had thought before I was a vampire that my life wouldn't be conventional. I never wanted conventional. I guess you really do have to be careful what you wish for. Now I didn't want a conventional vampire life either, and by the look of Damien, neither did he.

"If you're willing to learn, it would be a pleasure."

I sat with Damien on the sofa and my head sank into his shoulder. Sleep fell heavy on me, and that night I actually felt at peace.

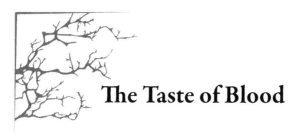

The Taste of Blood

Anthony

THE FOLLOWING NIGHT I walked through the city alone, still numb at losing Rachel. Heat flushed through my body and I realised I was bracing, all my limbs tense with anger.

Too wrapped up in my sorrow to notice, until I was dumbfounded at what I saw before me. Jolting out of self-pity, I watched, unable to move away, powerless to stop staring even though danger was in my face.

In the hidden corners of the city under the Neo-Classical columns, vampires and nephilim wrapped in an esoteric kiss of death. The vampires could not taste the blood of these vengeful angels though some had tried. Their screams sharp and piercing as they burned in agony, the delectable angelic blood scalding their insides. I watched the horror, the ecstasy and the brutality of two species coming together, which before this would have fought to the death, now entranced by blood, both attracted by the other. By the danger, the illicit temptation.

Some vampires used their eerie charms to subdue the hungry nephilim and enjoy the carnal pleasures that these creatures bestowed. Wicked and debauched, the fallen were ardent lovers and the vampires drunk up all the sensuality they could take. The struggle my kin had though was fierce. It is the strongest will in the world that in the moment of pleasure, to *not* drink blood, but some vampires enjoyed the denial that would save their lives. It was like looking at a scene straight out of Dante's Inferno.

It was shocking and carnal, my pulse raced, lust flooded my body, my need for blood.

Wayward nephilim stole the blood of vampires, the beautiful immortals merging in a bloody orgy, some willing, others taken by force. Those nephilim once so proud and pure now corrupt with the devilish fluid of the damned, their white wings stained black and their untainted splendour now a sublime and sinister elegance. I watched them, taking care not to be seen, and the intensity of their passion was overwhelming.

Behind the honey-coloured pillars, I watched the diabolical scene of fallen angels feasting on the once bold vampires. As I saw the frailty of the vampire compared to these creatures, their force and their indomitable spirit, I pitied them. Sensation turned to anger at this rape on my species. But was this not ironic? Did we not do the very same to mortals? I myself had taken pleasure in using my charms and then stealing blood of humans to satiate my hunger. I had stolen their virtues, and God only knew the outcomes I had left with the mortals of my past discretions. But this was violent, forceful, and beyond control.

A nephilim male, once tall and proud, bent over onto a vampire's neck as she struggled to stand, grabbing at the rough stone wall next to her as his brute strength unintentionally forced her downwards. I caught her eye as she screamed in terror of his overbearing power ripping her soul from her, fast and brutal.

Too late, she was gone and was swiftly dropped to the ground. He tilted his head, arching his back as if not to spill a drop of that precious fluid, then he suddenly flipped and doubled forward with the ferocity of the change. A wild howl from him sent me behind the cover of my hiding place, but my curiosity would not be repressed so I peeked from behind the pillar to look at him again.

His sweating, dark mass appeared vulnerable in his semi-naked state. He had drained his victim, her corpse lay on the pavement beside him. Yet, naked and exposed as he was, an intense energy emitted from him. Had I been an ordinary vampire I wouldn't have stood a chance.

To my surprise, Nathaniel appeared by my side and instinctively we approached this once Divine warrior. Nathaniel had recovered well and looked almost his normal self again. But I was too distracted by the scene in front of me and my intention too set to consider him much. Nathaniel watched in wonder having never been so close before to a creature like this. If he had, I doubt he would have lived to tell of it. The angel was so engrossed in his new sensations to take any notice of us or to perceive us as a threat. Had I not had the blood of those greater than me, he would've been right. *Don't abuse the power,* Emidius had told me.

Nathaniel grinned at me and I grinned back. He was predictable and I knew what he was thinking.

The depraved angel now on his knees, agony filling his core as his body experienced these new sensations and, ironically, just as his victim had done, he pawed at the walls to stay upright.

I walked over to him, his grey eyes looked darker now, almost black and his contorted face displaying all the sensations of his victim's blood coursing through his veins. I walked in front of him, calm and comforting. I crouched down and placed my hand on his face and smiled. Relief filled his face but in an instant it was me at his neck, my lips upon his skin as my teeth sunk in and I drank his blood.

He struggled, hapless fool. Kill my kin, what do you expect? I felt intense, vengeful, and heady all at once. For a few seconds I had to try and keep my feet beneath me while around me in all the corners of the city, chaos reigned.

As I stood back from him, the shock filled his face and I looked him in the eyes. A vampire drinking his blood with no ill effect was the last thing he expected and we shared that moment before his death.

I stumbled from being blood-drunk and Nathaniel steadied me, keeping his hands on the back of my shoulders as I locked my gaze on this immortal. He reached out to grab my hand, probably to drag me into the depths of Hell with him, but I stood back offended that such a creature would imagine me to care. I had struck back.

I swayed. My head felt like it was swimming and my body tingled and flushed hot all over.

Watching him without remorse as he crumpled into a ball and then fire sparked ferociously from him, white and hot. The instant heat and brightness stunned us and we instinctively jumped back. And then he was no more. Nothing surprised me anymore.

Before I moved away, I felt Marcus's presence rush up to me, and standing there looking at the scorch mark on the ground he said nothing. In the pandemonium around me, everything seemed in slow motion.

With that nephilim's blood rushing in me, forceful and intense.

"There are more than nephilim here, aren't there? I sense something else. Demons?"

"They are here, watching in the shadows."

Without another word, I moved unsteadily to the small hexagonal Georgian building that housed an ancient hot spring that was now Spa baths.

I gently pulled out what looked like a woman, but I knew was in fact a demon. She was hesitant; after all such species don't normally mix.

Her long slender white arms looked luminous under the street lamps and she was cold and fragile. Though from what I'd been told she was anything but.

Marcus stepped forward with Nathaniel, poised to attack, knowing the power these creatures have, and I stood there for a few seconds transfixed in her demonic spell.

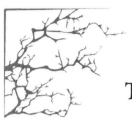

The Demon

Anthony

SHE SHUFFLED HERSELF, unsure of the situation. A nephilim and two vampires facing her, cornering her. Long dark hair fell down to her shoulders and her body was small and lithe. Her face milky white with sharp features and jet black eyes She looked like a *vision* of a human rather than a human—too perfect. Clenching her jaw, she muttered some spell in a language I couldn't understand. I still held her wrist; she looked at it, to me, and spat some words which I didn't recognise. Marcus was immediately at my side, talking back to her in an unknown language and had grabbed her other wrist.

I reminded myself that she was a demon, like the one in Rachel's home. The one looking to take my beloved. My dazed mind longed for Rachel then, and I felt a surge of emptiness without her. Shaking my head I focused on the demon in front of me, shoving all thoughts of Rachel aside.

"Who are you?"

She didn't respond but edged slowly away, Marcus and I still holding her wrists. I knew from what Marcus had said, most were stronger than vampires. But I am no ordinary vampire, as she would have seen from her hiding place.

"I need to know. I need to know about your kind."

She frowned, then lowered her eyebrows as if my questions were too simple to answer. "And why should I answer you?"

I shook my head. "Because you are here, and if you don't answer me, I will kill you."

Laughing, she cried, "You cannot kill a demon, vampire. We are not made the same as you! We can change if we will it, into the nonphysical."

I knew she was bluffing me. If that were true then she wouldn't be here right now talking to me. She quickly changed the subject. "Vampires and nephilim, what craziness is this? You should be more concerned with other entities. The streets are rich with devilry, with blood. There are worse fiends out tonight than demons."

Some strange compulsion drove me forward, and seconds later I held her wrist to my mouth and drank. She gasped in horror and I was vaguely aware of Nathaniel stepping up to me in shock. Marcus stood there, still clutching her wrist, his mouth open, I supposed not believing what he was seeing.

My instinct, to know her secrets that were held in her blood held. I always knew a being from their blood—their experiences, their confidences, their sins and their hopes. As I drink it, all is revealed to me in a flash of images or emotions.

Demon blood, like the nephilim, sent a tremor through me and not only did I see, I felt her life. Monstrous, deceitful, and merciless. In my mind I saw a void of black, a dimension of eternal nothingness, then a spark of a thought, and finally her. What I felt was her presence shifting from nothing to physical, filled with anger from having to rely on a mortal to come into existence. So to exist a demon relies on a mortal to acknowledge their presence, but once that mortal dies then the demon can no longer take physical form and shifts back into incorporeal. But with the veil shifted, many were seizing the opportunity to plough forth into the physical reality of men. With the chaos, the darkness growing in the hearts of man, their hate manifesting as wraiths, the demons had seized that energy, that hatred, and rode it like a wave into the twenty-first century.

I released my grasp and stumbled backwards to the ground, my body searing with burning liquid and her life flashing before me. In my haze I saw a great bright flash of green light and felt a tremor but, as darkness closed in on me, one piece of knowledge slammed into me. How to kill a demon.

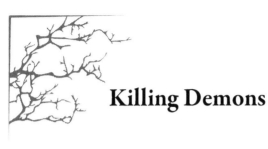

Killing Demons

Anthony

"WHAT HAPPENED TO ME? Her blood?"

"Yes," Marcus spoke. He got up and walked to me, ushering the others out looking concerned.

"Tell me of Lucius," I asked.

"Lucius is young for a demon, but he has the energy of a thousand minds made manifest by the realization of his being. He is physical to be sure, but if you don't acknowledge his existence, he cannot *be* in your reality. That's why he would be grateful to Aaron. Aaron made you aware of him and thus, he now exists in your reality."

Everything fell silent, I was too stupefied to speak. Why the fuck did Aaron do that?

I knew I'd kill him, that demon. I lay back and shut my eyes. Prickling and burning sensations ran through my body, no doubt from the nephilim and demon blood. I guessed I should be more careful in the future.

"Try and rest. You have pushed yourself too far this time. Yes, we know you can go further than most, but none has drunk the blood of a demon. Please stop drinking blood of creatures you know nothing about. You will get yourself killed or worse," Marcus sniggered.

I could believe him. My head was spinning and all I wanted to do was sleep. But every time I closed my eyes my head only seemed to spin faster. I remembered hating that feeling as a mortal. It seemed worse now.

"What could be worse than death?"

Marcus grunted in surprise. "Well, let me think. Living a life in purgatory as a strange ghoul type being, being neither alive nor dead and having no control over your destiny? Will that do? Is that worse?"

"Maybe not if I felt better as a ghoul!"

Acacius had come to see me. He was unblemished by what was occurring and he appeared unfazed by it, though I doubt he really was. His manner was annoyingly calm and sarcastic. He never participated in anything ungodly, unlike the rest of us. I had a gut feeling that would be his saving grace, and possibly my undoing.

"I like being around you and Anthony. You're always in the thick of the action. Killing a nephilim after drinking his blood! I should kill you, you know. But I won't. Dominic—the one you killed—had fallen from the path and death was his own making. But you! I am afraid for your soul, Anthony. You have fallen so far!"

"Acacius, I am weary and I don't care what you think. My soul? It's a bit late for that! My soul was lost the moment I first stole blood and killed an innocent. And yet, I am still here, damned or not. Why did you come here? To see, to feel perhaps? Feeling is something you never allow yourself to do."

"I *do* feel, Anthony, but I don't need to live my life in such an extravagantly debauched way as you do. I know... Vampires, act first, think later. Isn't that your motto?" he snapped.

I was annoyed that he came into my home to criticize me. He picked up on this and paused, looking out of the window at the dirty, busy road below and the grim cloudy weather. Then he turned to me and said, "So, the female demon; how was she?"

"How would you know that?" Unable to curb my fascination, I asked, my voice raised, "And how do you know so much about me? And why do you care?"

"Initially I didn't much. We hear of most that are turned. Especially by the foul creatures that turned you. They've been alluding us for years. I was more interested last year when I heard of the attack on Alexander, Tyrell's son. A vampire brazen enough to attack one of the Elite! That really grabbed my attention. But not as much as Emidius saving you. Then I knew I had to find you."

"You never told me that before."

"I don't tell you everything. But we heard, and then Marcus fell from grace. I knew he'd look to her for help, and that led me to you."

I felt really weary and didn't want this conversation now, but as he wouldn't leave I had to say, "But Emidius saved Alexander. Don't you think that's sick? I mean he was so vile, so cruel, and yet she of all creatures restored his life. I don't understand her, nor do I revere her. To save the son of Tyrell, that bastard despot? She is welcome to kill me for saying that."

"She acts in ways which you don't see the whole picture, Anthony. Tyrell was a despot, but there have been worse. *Better the devil you know.* You and your friend killed Alexander anyway, and Tyrell. They haven't set up a new order as far as I have found out. I suspect she knew his time was near."

"And me, you see me as a threat?"

"On the contrary. Are you not curious to see how this plays out? Nephilim bleeding vampires; what are the consequences? The two species have never mixed let alone shared blood and sex. And the demons... Ah, they have come out of the shadows. And still hiding but watching, the lycans lurk, biding their time and awaiting their opportunity."

He sat down on a chair in my room, thumbing over the books on the bookcase, and then looking at me, he spoke quietly, "I hear you're thinking... you're wondering if she annihilated the experimentals?"

I nodded. Had Emidius done that? We never knew. I almost died trying to do that myself.

"Well she didn't, we did. It was a brutal battle, but most of the creatures were exterminated. Except one. He reached the woods where the lycans are so we couldn't kill it, but we plan to soon."

Fallen Angels

Lucius

"WE HAVE NO LIMITS, Lucius; I wonder why you choose her. I did once, and look what she did to me," Nathaniel asked me.

"You *allowed* her to stake you! You know full well her power is nothing compared to yours. You wanted that experience, you felt in that moment ready to let go, but you could not. I swear to God, Nathaniel, you're a crazy bastard. Why did you do that? You stop at nothing to experience new sensations, it is a wonder you're still alive.

"But here you are alive, just, and I have to say, my old friend, you're not looking too bad for someone who was doused in petrol and staked. Me, I like a challenge, weak subordinate women are for feeble men, and I am not that. I love the fact that she was brazen enough to try and kill you, she invigorates me. But her heart, her soul is so untainted and for one who has fallen into darkness that *is* rare. She is mine, she will bear my son and we will raise him together, that is my wish. And I always get what I want, however long it takes."

92

"What about Damien? I would not see any harm come to my cousin. She and him have bonded - though she's doesn't yet know the truth of him. That bond is rare it cannot easily be undone."

"Yes, he is a problem I hadn't counted on. And as he's your kin, though he doesn't know it, I can't kill him. I think I may leave him to you and your charms to persuade him that his feelings should lie elsewhere."

"You're asking me to seduce my own cousin?"

"Nathaniel, you'd seduce your own kin without hesitation, and it's not as if you're blood line is direct. Just do it enough to steer him away from her."

"I see," he grinned. "But it won't work, they've bonded. You don't understand that with us, once it's done that's it."

"You said it's not easily undone, meaning there is a way, what way is that?"

"Death of one of them is usually the way. I suggest you leave my kin out of this, get your child with another and leave that woman to her own downfall. I've known you long enough and I've never seen you smitten like this, I fear it will be you who is damned this time. Damien is far more powerful than you think, he passes as a normal immortal and he lives humbly, but let me assure you, his power easily surpasses mine. You know nothing of his Maker. I'm done with this talk, we were meant to be having fun and thanks to Anthony's sympathy for my situation, and his blood I am dying to taste an angel. Or two."

"You really think you won't be harmed? If you're wrong..."

"I won't be, he wasn't and I drank enough from him. Come on, let's look."

I led my vampire friend into the city and it didn't take us long to come across a nephilim male high on vampire blood. Of course, as is the way with the blood lust, the inexperienced angel was aroused, drunk and all over the place. He could barely stand, he looked like a human who had drunk way too much alcohol, it was funny to watch, and dangerous. Nathaniel walked carefully towards him and stared at him. He slumped down against a wall his eyes glazed and we both heard his heart pounding so fast we thought he might hyperventilate. At least he was still dressed; this was obviously his first time with a vampire. Nathaniel knew the vampire woman. He knows all the vampires in this small city.

"Sarah," he whispered. Her eyes were glazed from the ferocity of the male drinking from her. If Nathaniel didn't help her now, she'd be dead soon. He pushed the drunk angel aside and bit his wrist for her. She gulped as fiercely as she could; drinking for her life and within a few minutes she looked almost restored. He stayed there with her, his arms around her until he knew she was alright. We are not always so merciless.

Me, I was taunting the angel, whispering in his ear and running my demon fingers through the fallen one's hair.

Actually Marcus was Nathaniel's goal for that evening. But what could we do?

Viewing our winged friend at last and without a word, Nathaniel went over to him, pressed his cold body against his, and whispered death in his ear and then bit his neck. I watched as he drank his blood, rapturous; euphoric. Nathaniel's eyes widened, and I worried then that the fiery liquid was burning him.

I steadied him and tried to bring him around, but he was out of it. Lost in a stupor, vulnerable and warm with that liquid burning through him.

Within minutes of drinking, the angel was in a daze, doubled up on the floor, groaning. I flinched back, pulling Nathaniel away, who had in his blood lust sunk to his heels, his legs kicking erratically. Hauling Nathaniel up, he was so high on blood he fell back into me and flinched in shock as the angel ignited a brilliant blue-white light, immense heat almost scorching us. Shielding our faces and Sarah who was by now as I recall, walking in the distance turned to look.

In the seconds that followed, the fallen one was gone with just ash left where he had been. A sweat broke out over my friend and his face paler than usual, his hands, body trembling. Blinking rapidly the heat of his blood was burning me, he tried to talk, but only managed to mumble, "Anthony," before pain seized him and he crumpled over.

I called him and didn't say who I was, only a friend of Nathaniel's and waited until Anthony arrived.

Anthony swiftly gave Nathaniel his blood, he drank intensely, hoping for relief.

To say that Anthony was furious with me is an understatement; he swore to kill me, whilst my friend drank his blood. Little did Anthony know that I had known Nathaniel for a century and I had possibly just saved Rachel from an eternity with him. But he didn't need to know that.

Nathaniel whispered to Anthony, his voice croaking, "Why did it burn me, but not you?" He seemed slightly better, still too warm inside but cooler than earlier. "I don't know, maybe because mine is purer? I mean it came directly from her. Don't worry about that now, just rest."

As Anthony stood up, he looked at me, his eyes narrow, he sneered, "If you go near her, I vow I will hunt you down and you will beg for death."

He left, taking Nathaniel with him, his arms wrapped around Nathaniel's shoulders, aiding him. As for me, I went to find her. I enjoy the hunt.

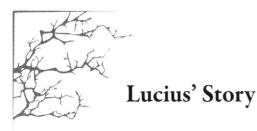

Lucius' Story

Lucius

I GLIDED OVER THE BED, hovering over Rachel's body. Aaron had made the fatal mistake of revealing my presence to her so now she was aware of me. I had been watching as she slept night after night, when she and her 'lover' returned from the hunt. But that was over now. He was emotionally attached to Nathaniel, my wicked friend and debaucher of dreams. Which left her for me. A new vampire, capable of...

She opened her eyes as if sensing my presence and at the moment she was conscious of me, our eyes met and I transformed from spiritual to physical. I am only made real by the awareness, the recognition of the minds of the living, and so spirit becomes flesh. At last I was able to embrace my lover, whom I had watched for many weeks.

I am the darkness to her light. Her scent, her smile have a hold over me and *her* soul draws my savage soul screaming towards it. In all my years I have never felt a yearning, a desire so strong as this. And yet the brutal truth that a demon and a vampire have never been together before causes me doubt. Despite this doubt, she is mine and I shall never leave her. We will be for all eternity, my demonic blood mixing with hers so immortality will embrace us together, forever.

To touch her is exquisite. She seems unaware that I am real, she thinks that she is dreaming. Her sighs ignite sensations in my body that had dulled over time. So many women, the experience had deadened beyond imagining. But a vampire, everything is heightened, every pulse felt stronger, scent sweeter, and kiss more powerful.

Her hazel eyes seemed to darken in passion and her lips, so soft against mine. I feel young again, like when I first experienced passion—that mixture of excitement and intense anticipation. She is my light, my blood.

He left without sensing my presence and so I lay there beside her while she was somewhere between sleep and wakefulness, believing she is dreaming and that I am not real. I'm not offended. With her lover gone she needs time to adjust and in time I will take his place. I will defend her fiercely unlike Anthony, and unlike him my emotions are stable, for a demon at least. Her head on the pillow, her eyes looked tired as she drifted back to sleep and I wrapped myself around her.

I was fiercely happy that Marcus had fallen and watched with interest the others that were following him. Their righteous world had started to crumble, but I was no fool. I would not stay around long enough to get pulled down with them.

For centuries I had lived in fear of those winged vigilantes and watched my step, my only defence my speed to save me from their uncompromising lack of mercy. My kind had hidden in the shadows, made to feel revulsion of our species for our lust for human souls, making me livid and petulant.

I had, in the beginning, tried to get my own retribution but that nearly cost me my life. Outwitting them by de-materializing was my only hope then. Then they sought me out, for years. Every night I would end up either running or vanishing, and every time I vanish, my power wanes, as they intended.

For so long I was forced to exist as an outlaw on this Earth, or in the plane above it as an outcast judged by those who deem themselves a higher authority than I, even though they are cast out and damned by their God and then they sought to damn me. Nephilim are God's fallen angels, descendants of those he sent to Earth as punishment, no longer allowed to stay in the realms of Heaven.

Righteous fools, I watched with wonder and exhilaration at their demise. As their morals faltered and crumbled, my happiness grew. Now my kin could rise and be part of this society, this modern age so easily corrupted, capturing the souls of the dispossessed.

And with my vampire lover, I felt at last like my time had come, my turn to stand tall as the angels around me faltered and ceased. As the fallen ones drink vampire blood I knew their ruin is imminent.

Her though. I had searched for centuries and though I have had many human lovers, I have never had one like her—a vampire. A vampire with a pure soul. I wanted to be near that, near her.

I am a vicious and calculating creature by nature, but something in me is drawn to her. I contemplated this for many hours, I had never questioned my nature before. And to question it over a woman, my gut reaction is one of ruin. But she will bear my son, of that I was sure. She has the blood of the demi-god in her, after drinking from him, and so shall he, my son.

I would die for this... Soon I shall reveal my true existence to her and she will know I am real, but for now I shall let her dream.

Most call me a devil, but I am not *He*. I am, however, an Incubus, a demon. So many species in the underworld of darkness, we wait for you to falter just a little. Believe in us, and we can consume you.

I cast many under my spell, drawing them into my world of darkness and depravity. I devour the souls of the living, feeding on these to strengthen my life force. Human kind becomes predicable with time. So I preyed on the less willing, and that made it more interesting for me. But many now don't believe in the supernatural. That makes it harder.

I enjoy interacting with mortals, their feelings, their emotions, taking liberties. I look so young to them. One thing that never ceases to amuse me is their shock when they discover how strong, how powerful I am. I have taken thousands of souls into my being which has slowly increased my strength.

There are many supernaturals now. I have to be more careful. If anything they are my only threat. The new-borns from the dark world are usually no threat as they cannot detect me and I enjoy toying with them, but I still need my wits about me. Though some are my friends and we even hunt together. Nathaniel is one of these. He was always a rebel. Rules cannot contain him.

This is why we got on so famously; his disregard for rules and my blatant lack of respect for anything higher or not in my own interest seems to have bonded us.

I have fathered many children during my time but none have become powerful as was my desire and intent. I am ever hopeful that one of these will be the greatest necromancer of all time. And so, with Rachel, I will try again...

Time has no meaning to me; it is only relevant to mortals. I exist and I am everything and nothing. I am conjured by the power of your belief in me. As soon as you accept my existence, I enter yours...

Reflective World

Rachel

I CLOSED MY EYES AND allowed him to consume me in passion. Was he real? He felt like a dream, a dream without consequences. Feeling his desire, his touch, his presence consumed me

"Rachel, your heart is pure for a vampire. I want to show you this place and to be with you for all time. You will find I am devoted to you and my heart, demonic though it is, will never waver. I just want you," he whispered.

And so, I held my fantasy close. Anthony had already left. Damien was all I wanted now, but this dream, this was erotic. Who was the man in my dream? The demon, Lucius? If I was dreaming of a demon, had he snuck his way into my subconscious? Maybe, but it was such a sensual dream, safer than reality. And in my slumber Lucius wrapped himself around me. I heard him whisper in my ear, felt his touch on my skin. I'm not sure I want to wake up.

Suddenly I jolted, my stomach flipped, and I felt like I was being pulled. It was so strong I couldn't open my eyes, I held onto him with trepidation. A fast, warm wind blew past us, pushing against me, peeking through half-open eyes to see I was no longer in my bedroom. I was in what looked like a tunnel. Clinging tighter to this creature as I was being swept to God knows where, my body froze in fear.

Trying to hide my utter shock, I somehow managed to pull myself together in an instant by schooling my facial expression and fighting against my body to look relaxed. I'd had an inkling before, but in my half-sleep state had ignored it and assumed that it was just a dream.

An icy chill swept over me as fear rose from the pit of my stomach and I lost my breath for a second. But there was Lucius, smiling warmly and trying to put me at ease. Who knew a demon could do that?

"Where are we?" was all I could say, straining to maintain composure.

"Come, see." He got up with such grace and offered me his hand.

He looked young, about nineteen, and his long black hair hung straight matching his dark eye brows. His eyes, though small, looked kind and his lips, I had tasted those lips. His lithe body was covered in tattoos—skulls, patterns in black and white, and some full colour. Writing was also inked on him, but I couldn't read it. My guess was he was Native American in origin. He looked like he belonged to a gang. He wore an old black T-shirt and blue jeans, he was bare foot. Noticing me noticing him, he spoke quietly. "Ah, no shoes! Shoes stop our connection to the Earth. I like to feel connected."

I nodded. A breeze swept through blowing back his hair and the sky...the sky... Hues of red and bronze in the sky, smudged from light at the horizon with the sinking sun fading into dark, added an ethereal glow to the trees. Ivy was bright, illuminated under that warm ruby sunset and amber leaves created an inviting warm carpet. The whole place had an unearthly feel. It was calming and I felt immediately at ease, like I would never want to leave this place.

In the distance willow trees arched together, their branches intertwined looking like a natural passage way. Someone had placed lanterns hanging from the branches. The golden leaves hung heavy with water droplets as if it had dewed recently and a scattering of them had fallen to the ground. As I looked beyond I saw the russet reds, greens, and copper tones of a forest, thick and plush.

The rich scent in the air, pierced with a hint of cold stimulated my senses, saturated as they already were. How had Lucius found this place? It didn't look the sort of place to find a demon hiding. I had underestimated him, and I felt sure that there was more to him than a stealer of souls. This being must have a soul himself to want to be in such a beautiful place.

Stillness hung heavy around us. No sounds penetrated that stillness. Finding my breath after this surprise, I asked again breaking the silence, "Where are we?"

With a huge glowing smile, he looked into my eyes. "This is my sanctuary. I have never shared it with another, but I have come here for decades when I needed to escape. Allow me to lead you to my home." He looked like a boy at that moment, proudly showing off his creation. "It is humble and basic. I come here to get away from the human world, from other immortals. I come here to read, to study, and to rest. I don't know where we are. It's a portal. That's all I know. There are many portals. I can show you them, but this is my favourite one and where I call home. Demons—well, at least me—don't spend all our time tormenting humans and supernaturals! That would be boring! I can only speak for myself and my sister."

"You have a sister? Is she here?" I asked, trying not to sound anxious.

"No, I have never brought her here. And I haven't seen her for many years."

"So, how does that work? You must then have parents?"

"Not as such. We come from split energy, from the same mind of creation—the being that created us into reality. But we never speak of it."

I was feeling unsteady with so much to take in. A portal, a demon who reads, a sister. I looked around searching for others, thinking surely we would not be alone here.

He offered me his hand which I did not want, but I took as I wanted him to feel at ease with me. And my legs, my body were shaken from this weird reality. Walking together he put his arm around me and led the way.

I had to take a deep breath and concentrate so that I didn't flinch. The difference when a fantasy becomes a reality.

"There are creatures here, Rachel. Many. They're mostly shy and I have never known any to be harmful. They're not like creatures from the world you're used to. They are more unusual, dark, spectacular even. I find it all, and them, very fascinating."

I knew I should be afraid, and that I should be trying to get back. But I didn't. For once I felt at peace with this place, even if not with him.

It was beautiful. The red glow of the atmosphere, the walkway of twisted hazel trees that led us to his stone cottage and the small, lithe black creatures I caught in the corner of my eye who were spying at our presence and darting back so as not to be seen. They didn't feel like a threat to me at all.

His home was like a cabin from a fairy-tale. Made of logs with a thatch roof and a small stone chimney topping it. It was small, rectangular with a little stone wall around it that contained a garden.

"I promise you that you will be safe here, and I will always endeavour to keep you safe."

I looked at him then. I stopped in the middle of the path, just before we'd reached his cottage. His dark, almost black eyes were sincere. His black hair flopped over his forehead in an almost boyish way that enhanced how handsome his face was. I almost pushed the lock of hair away, but I stopped myself. My need to ask this question burned brighter than my desire to touch his hair. "But why? Why me? What do you want from me?"

He looked taken aback. "I love you, of course. I have watched you for weeks, sensed you, your heart, your feelings, your loneliness. I love you and I want to be with you. We shall have a child, a son of course. He will become a powerful necromancer. We will be together forever."

My heart sank. Oh God... A demon was in love with me, kidnapped me to God knows where. I needed to get out of here. I needed to get away regardless of how serene it was. I wasn't about to fall in love with a creature that declared his heart to me after five minutes and kidnapped me. And a *child*?

But before I could think further he said, "We are connected you know. You and I, we have a shared energy. We are one."

He sounded sincere, for a psychotic demon, so I pressed him carefully. "Explain? I mean I am physical, a vampire, but you are, well I'm not sure who you are. Tell me, I want to know how demons come into existence."

I knew I had to play him, to learn as much as possible about him, where we were and how to get out of here. And he was all too willing to oblige me. Then again, I had been through this before with my Maker. And thank God he couldn't read minds!

"We demons don't come from the same dimension as you. We can only become physical when a human or immortal becomes aware of us. Before that we are just energy. How that happens, I don't know. We just exist as non-physical beings, but we are attracted to those who resonate on a similar energy, or of those who interest us.

"You interested me greatly. *A vampire.* Of course I have met many a vampire, but none quite as you. There is a purity about you, in your heart. So when those nephilim mentioned that I was in your home, and you became aware of me, I knew then that as soon as you accepted my existence I could become real to you. I had watched you for some time before, as I watched Anthony secretly helping Nathaniel—your enemy. And I knew you deserved better. Damien was cause for my concern, but not now. Now that you are with me, we have eternity to know each other."

Damien! How the hell did he know about him! Alarm bells were ringing so loud it was all I could do to compose myself. Dear God...

"So how do we get in and out of these portals?" His confidence in himself was my advantage, and he spilled forth information because of my demeanour. He didn't doubt me for a moment. He must have assumed he was stronger. Foolish creature.

"To get here, I used a dark mirror. I had to summon energy from within the mirror and focusing on travelling through the portal, you have to train your mind and your bodywork to do this because it has to be felt from within, on the place you want to go. There are other places, not on Earth but in different dimensions. There are portal entrances here, mirrors dotted around in the woodlands. You don't have to worry, I won't keep you prisoner here, I just needed to get us away from the nephilim."

And Damien. "What of the creatures here? Who are they, and why are they here?"

"They came, most likely, from your dimension. Some may have been left. They change into shadow over time. Their matter diminishes because of the pull or the energy difference. It's not wise to spend too long in a portal. I am no expert and have little interest in physics. In the main, they are harmless but some seem tortured. Probably those who've been left here."

"And you don't know who left them?"

"They were here before I arrived. I haven't met any others here, so I don't know. I have been to other portals in my lifetime and shadow creatures are often found there. But for their history, I don't know. It would be best to avoid them."

So then I knew, to get home I would need to find a mirror and *feel* like I was home. The other thing I knew then was that I needed to make contact with these shadow creatures, and help them get home in return for helping me. As for him, now he was physical, that part would be easy. I had to be balanced, not too nice and not nasty, to gain his trust. And that's exactly what I was doing.

His log cabin had two rooms, a little open fire and was sparsely furnished. He'd most likely built it himself, probably for his previous victim. It was clean which told me he'd used it recently and as he lit a fire I sat back pondering this incredulous experience.

"What do you eat?"

"We don't. Well, we live off of the energy of mortals. If you were mortal you'd no doubt think that awful, but under the circumstances..."

I had no idea what demon blood would do to me, maybe it would kill me. I knew the experience would not be good, but I knew no other way out. So I said, "What about me? I can hardly drink the blood of the others here. I know they have none and I am hungry. A hungry vampire is not something you want to experience!" I grinned trying to make it a joke, but to convey how serious I was.

He looked tentatively at me, slightly unsure but then he obviously felt he was confident in his judgement that he could trust me. He actually believed that I wanted to be with him, have his child. As if kidnapping and trapping someone was normal! I didn't know whether he was stupid or narcissistic. I wasn't about to find out.

"There are two choices, we could go back through the portal, but with our enemies there I don't recommend right now or...you could try me? I know your blood mixed with mine, we will have a son who is beyond any other. A powerful necromancer. As we will be together forever, we have to trust each other."

He walked forward to where I was sitting and knelt before me, moving his silky black hair away from his neck. Demon blood—I had no idea what affect this would have on me, but I also had no choice. Before my lips touched his neck, he moved his face and looked me in the eyes, a plea of trust. But I am a vampire and only a fool trusts a vampire.

"I have looked for you for centuries," he whispered so softly I almost missed it. I pitied him then, just for a second. And then I bit his neck.

He stiffened at first but I held him tenderly stroking his back and his arm lovingly, luring him into a false sense of sensuality. He seemed so fragile then, in my arms, and his blood was bitter and strong. Under normal circumstances I would've spat it out, but my life depended on me taking his. And that was the situation *he* had put me in. And so I drank.

Seconds later he realized his error and started struggling, but surprisingly for me, his strength was nothing compared to mine. I didn't understand that as the nephilim had said demons were stronger, maybe I was lucky that my maker was so old and so strong.

As I drank I experienced his emotions through his lifetime, they were wicked, terrible, he had feasted on the vulnerable, luring them in, using them and taking their life force, their soul, leaving them hollow and drained. These had been innocent souls, mainly women and some young men. I almost choked on that acrid blood filled with so much hate, violence, and maliciousness but I drew it in now, harshly. My head swam with his experiences and my grip was firm; he didn't stand a chance. This time he had picked on the wrong woman. Vampires are not for the faint hearted or the weak.

As I felt his black rotten heart stop I remained fixed on him, just to be sure. I dragged his lifeless body outside and as I built the pyre the Shadow creatures' peered out from their hiding places. I didn't stop to look at them, I was just aware of their presence.

One called to me, half hidden behind the tree line, its voice weak and high. "You'll have to cut off his head and tear out his heart before you burn it!"

"What?"

"He's a demon, fire alone may not kill his spirit. To be sure, you should do as I suggest."

I couldn't believe it, killing by drinking his blood was one thing. How the hell would I cut off his head and take out his heart! What a repulsive thought. It crossed my mind that this creature was teasing me.

"I don't have anything to do that with," I called back. To my amazement two of them crept forward, one carrying a large, curved silver dagger and the other a silver sword. They laid these near me and ran off like startled animals. I wanted to ask why they had these, who they were, but I also didn't want to hang around, in case this demon decided to rise from the dead.

Oh God, just do it. The dagger was beautiful with an ornate wooden handle and a silver blade that curved slightly, the light catching it like some Holy relic. Using the dagger I ripped open his shirt and paused. Taking blood is very different from this, but gritting my teeth I thrust the blade into him. It was worse than disgusting and the smell, putrid and strong. Tearing the flesh and pulling past the ribs, using all my strength, I pulled out his heart. It wasn't red, but black and it pumped sporadically in my hand causing me to jump. I cast it down in horror, grabbed the sword and hesitated. My hands were bloody and slippery, so I placed the sword next to me and grabbed up his shirt to wipe off his blood.

Divine give me strength, I knew that if I'd been mortal I wouldn't have had the emotional or physical strength for this, as it was tough. As his head separated, a fierce green light shot out and sent me backwards. For seconds it belted out, illuminating everything around me, and the shadow people hid in fear, though my gut told me this wasn't the first demon they had seen destroyed.

I was sent back off my feet and this light grew, brightening everything, intense heat warming me instantly. It shot up and blazed and a great crack like lightening then thunder reverberated around the wood. I was too dazed to move for a few seconds, spots and flashes blurred my sight from the intensity of the light.

I heard the shadow people creep slightly forward, and I wondered what effect this had on us all. Picking myself up, I brushed myself down then looked around for some dry sticks. I couldn't help but grin, my shadowy friends spied from the trees watching me intently.

Rubbing two sticks together I eventually got a flame, placing it on some tinder bundle and put this around the base of the pyre. I picked up his head and heart and placed it on. I smelt of his death, which I suppose was apt. I had sympathized with him, before I drank his blood and learned the story of his cruelty.

The flames caught his caustic body quickly and grew fiercely, within minutes creating an inferno so hot that I had to step back several paces. Nausea hit me, that putrid blood in my veins, and I fought against it. It had to make me stronger, had to.

And as I watched, standing back I was aware that others had joined me, keeping their distance but just watching. I felt no threat from them, as he had suggested. Maybe because they knew I could not really harm them since they seemed almost diaphanous. Like ghosts, their shadow forms started to emerge and soon I saw dozens of them creeping around the tree lines, shadows within shadows.

I turned slowly to address them and most slunk back, hiding so I spoke softly.

"I did not come here of my own will but was kidnapped here by him, a taker of souls and maker of lies. I need to find the mirrors to get home, those who can help me; I will gladly take with me."

Not a creature stirred. "I mean you no harm; I just want to get home. Who can help? Who also wants to return home?" No answer. I turned to watch him burn, he had seemed crazy but not evil. He'd hidden that maliciousness well, maybe because he knew I was strong. Had I been weaker, he probably would've treated me badly as he'd done with the others.

A shrill voice replied, "We don't know if we can trust you. Anyway, our home may not be the same as yours, there are many channels leading to different portals."

"I come from Earth. I have no quarrel with you, but it saddens me that you may be stuck here as I am, and may want to get home."

"Time is different here, you think you've been here a day or so, but out there, it could be years."

"So you'd rather stay here, fading? You don't even want the chance to see, to get back?"

Murmurs amongst them filled the quiet night and a flock of shadow birds landed on the tree above me. To my surprise they spoke.

"We will help. We don't know if it's possible but we can try. We know of the mirrors you seek, but they are not near."

As they finished, another voice from a spindly tall creature in the shape of a human, stepped forth with others behind it. "We, too, shall help. Some here regard this place as home, those like him." And it pointed to the burning remains of Lucius. "They come here with their foul, cruel ways bringing those against their will. But others prefer it; it is peaceful in the main. I know some wish to leave and yearn for home. I believe you. You cannot easily harm us, for we have no blood. You will starve here if you stay and in that starvation madness will consume you. So we will come."

I felt relieved. Not only could I get home, though God knows what year it might be when I return, but I could help others, too. Even if we failed, at least we tried which was better than doing nothing.

The birds led the way, flying above us through the dark, tangled wood, the leaves crunching under my feet. They were a small flock and I wondered how they'd got here. They told me that they were sent here by a necromancer. As they were crows he had tried to use them for his magic. They, like the others, didn't know how long they'd been here, possibly years. One thing was common—they had all arrived here against their will.

The land nurtured no living things here. When I asked about the trees and plants they told me they were suspended, in a perpetual state of autumn. The whole place had an eerie silence to it.

The scenery around us shimmered and bent in the strange red light, like walking through glass, yet things looked normal, until I looked too close or glanced at the shadow creatures around me. This world was also too still, too quiet. Except for our small travelling party, nothing moved. I was warm and I wasn't sure if it was the demon blood or the temperature. Whatever the case, I was ready to escape this place where everything appeared normal, but wasn't.

After I'd fought the initial nausea from drinking Lucius's blood, I felt stronger than ever with a wild energy running through me like nature, rushing and forceful. It took all my will to control this and keep my focus. This energy was surging, and at times I felt lightheaded and distracted.

I tried not to stare and they didn't seem keen on talking. There were a dozen that came with me, the birds above cawed, but these creatures only whispered amongst themselves.

Time passed and the dark orange sun began to crest the horizon and the air felt crisp and clean. The wood seemed never ending, but it was beautiful and I knew then at some point I would venture back when I understood how to travel here properly.

One of the birds swooped down and landed on a low branch just ahead of me. "We should be nearing the place now. You'll see a large mirror in the woods, near a gate," it cawed.

I nodded, I wasn't sure whether it had spoken words to me, or whether I now understood it's cawing. I hoped it was the latter. I hoped this was a new gift I had received.

I wanted to know how and why a large mirror would end up here, but all of this was beyond my comprehension. Magic would be the answer so I didn't bother to ask. It was fascinating in this place, and with Lucius's blood in me I seemed more alert to the scent in the air, the slight changes in direction of the wind.

Despite this awareness, this world seemed empty. The tapping of insects was silent and the tiny rustles of animals in the woods were non-existent. These sounds were as familiar to me as my own heartbeat, the woods being my favourite refuge, yet here in this dimension, they were gone and I missed them.

I was lost in thought as we walked along, but gradually I sensed the growing excitement of the shadow creatures. The sky once again was growing dark and the beautiful hues of orange gold surrounded inky black clouds. Despite the increasing excitement, part of me was sad as I continued to enjoy the scenery around me. The emptiness of this land weighed heavily on my heart. As I thought this, the crows and the shadow creatures grew louder and their footsteps and beating of their wings became more frenzied. I looked up to see a mirror.

The forest was almost completely dark and was so dense that the mirror was partially hidden, covered with bracken and golden leaves. In front of it lay a sprinkling of fairy ring mushrooms. The last of the sun hit the glass so a thin slither of light shone out. The edge was gold leaf, thick and arched. It was surreal to see this in the middle of a wood.

As everyone arrived at the mirror, all the shadow creatures surrounded it and silence fell. I gulped and my mouth went dry as I knew they were all depending on me. I sat down on the leaf littered ground to gather some courage and calm my racing thoughts.

"Well, vampire, what now?" The bird's voice was urgent with fear.

"Lucius told me we have to build up the energy with a strong intention of where we want to go. I can feel this place is enchanted, can you?" There was a silence as all tried to tap into the magic here. It was strong to be sure.

We were all gathered around the mirror, some stuck to the trees, others crouched or sat near me by the mirror. The birds nestled on the low branches above us as night crept in on us. We were at an edge of the forest, an edge that had been lost long ago. Behind a small iron gate, a scattering of trees led away to what looked like fields in the dimming light. The mirror leaned against the gate.

"But who'll go first?" one of the shadow people asked, his voice slightly strangled in worry.

"You can, if you wish. I will make sure that you're all safely through. I don't know where you have all come from. If it's Earth, you could all concentrate on that, feel like we are already there, link hands and go together. You birds could perch on our shoulders? But...we have to concentrate, all of us on the same thing at the same time. As those passing through, we cannot afford fear to break our focus, otherwise we could all be lost, separated and end up God knows where! So if you want to do that, we need to take a little time to ready ourselves. There may be no going back, and this could be our only chance. That is the best suggestion I can think of."

Again they murmured amongst themselves and I could feel their anticipation, it was almost tangible. I sat there imagining being home, but I thought it better to just imagine being in Bath, lest we all spill forth into my little house!

At length when the last of light had almost gone, one came forward. "We are agreed, although we don't all know where each of us comes from. We shall imagine and feel being there and concentrate on that alone. Either way, we will have tried. Linking hands sounds the best idea. But we think it better to start as the sun rises, and not when it sinks."

I smiled. That sounded a good plan. Although I find nature quite impatient, it would be easier for all of us to have none waiting alone in the dark in that beautiful and haunting place.

"Are we sure we have left none behind?" I suddenly had a terrible feeling that others could be lost here. For some reason I felt terribly protective about leaving any others behind.

"We see all that have come through, and except under worlders, we know them all. This is all of us." His words were kind and sounded genuine.

With his words, I nodded and felt some relief. I looked around and noticed many of the creatures bedding down under the trees, building a fire to share while the birds nested in the trees. For the first time since I got there, happiness filled the air and some even laughed, tentatively. I supposed that they had lived in fear and isolation for so long and never believed they could access this portal.

"Have none of you ever tried to use this portal before?"

"Of course, many, many times, but all have failed. We didn't know what you told us. We were brought here by demons, necromancers, witches. Most were in shock, stolen from our beds or plucked from the sky, and when that shock wore off, there was no one to ask or spy on to discover how to use the portals. We still wonder why you help us."

"I'm sorry that you wonder that. I may be a vampire, perhaps because I am new, I still remember my humanity, my compassion. Over time, I have heard, once you've seen all your friends and family die, over time we can become detached. I strive not to be that."

The creature looked thoughtful.

Now I ventured to ask, "Do you mind me asking, who are you? What's your name?" I couldn't tell if the being was male or female. Its eyes, like my own had no colour in the irises. Its appearance was almost transparent. It looked forlorn with that question and I was about to reach out in comfort, but I thought better of it.

"I'm so sorry if I've upset you. If we're successful, I will try and help you. All of you."

It looked at me, eyes heavy with so much pain, as one does when you believed for so long that there was no hope. *No hope.* I cannot imagine the dread of that.

To my surprise, the creature answered, "I cannot really remember who I was, and I still find it hard to believe that you would help us. I thank you." It got up and sat with the others and I crawled closer to the fire and fell asleep. I hadn't slept at night for so long.

Dawn broke and the sunrise was unlike anything on Earth. Brilliant golden orange filled the sky and the cool air woke me.

Everyone was awake and looking to me to begin. Sadness once again gripped me to leave this place, but I got up and brushed myself down. Inhaling the pure sweet air, I knew it was now or never. Words weren't needed and one by one everyone gathered in a line before the mirror. A brilliant light caught the glass and shone like a beacon of hope on all of us as we stood before it. But it seemed there was some fear about who shall go first. That last step, filled with trepidation.

"I'll go last, to ensure everyone is through and safe. Who feels the strongest, the most desire to go through?"

Silence. Then the one who I spoke to the night before stepped forward. "I will go first, but where shall I think of? I cannot remember where I am from."

The others nodded and agreed and the birds squawked.

"I'll give you an image. Think of a park, green and lush surrounded by shrubs and trees. Hear the birds in the pale blue sky and the soft white clouds. Now think of the sounds of buzzing insects underfoot and people enjoying this place. See the flowers in your mind, reds, blues, greens, and smell their fragrance.

"At the entrance of this park is a huge stone obelisk with three stone lions lying down at its base, the whole monument surrounded by a balustrade, or small stone wall. Hold that vision, feel as if you're there, feel it in every part of your being. Hold onto that, however afraid, however unsettling. Just focus."

And then with the birds on our shoulders, our hands linked tightly, the energy peaked. The glass on the mirror melted and swam like liquid metal, that enchanted energy had come alive. As the first of the shadow people put his hand to the mirror, it moved like thick liquid, then we stepped through.

As the first one disappeared through, gasps came from my gossamer friends. Just before I stepped through I looked behind me, one last glance at that ethereal place where I had killed a demon and freed people. I would visit again, I knew in my heart. Then I focused on the monument, on the stone lions in the park and I stepped through.

As before, nothing seemed real, but this time I kept my eyes open. Whirling winds, like flying down a vertical tunnel and rainbow flashes of lights whizzed past me. I realized I was holding my breath, and then relaxed a little. It was fun, fast, and knowing where and when I wanted to arrive I had a sudden jolt of confidence.

Quicker than I could anticipate, I tumbled out onto the ground on one of the lawns of the park. I had managed to get them back to Bath. They had seen the park as I had wanted them to. All of us disoriented, none of us landed on our feet. Luckily, I think we arrived at night. They were just over a dozen.

Panic set in with most. Again I had to get into leader mode. Some were shaking, others were crying, some were calling hysterically. Their faces, eyes, and mouths were wide, open in shock and fear.

I raised my voice a little, to be heard over their commotion. "It is all right, we are here, in my home town. It's night time, that's all. Tomorrow the dawn will come and what you imagined will be real."

But now we'd arrived, new problems popped up. Were we in the right time? I didn't want to dwell on that. One of them protested, "But we don't know where we belong, or where we can go. Are we safe here?" Their faces were contorted with angst and they huddled like beasts afraid of the wolves. I would have to take all of them to my home. I hadn't really thought that through, but I had thought that I would ask Acacius as he would know and was compassionate enough to help.

"You can stay at my home. It *is* small and not too far and it's safe. We can..." I was about to say walk, but that was obvious anyway. Even in the park with limited lighting, my immortal eyes could see that they were more solid than before, but they seemed to shimmer from diaphanous to solid. The crows flew around, looking almost like they should now.

One of the crows came to me. "We will stay here for the night, but first we shall follow you so that we know how to find you."

I realised then, now back in my time that it didn't speak my language, rather that I understood. It's odd what we wish for. All my life I had wanted to communicate with animals. I got my wish but the circumstances were beyond anything I could've imagined.

Rachel Disappears

Anthony

I'D SPENT TIME AWAY from Rachel's home, and now she wasn't answering her phone which went straight to voice mail. I had a spare key so I went with Marcus to see if she was alright. I knew she was still angry at me, but I was worried. I had a really bad gut feeling and I needed to check she was alright, whatever the consequences.

As I walked into her home the stillness struck me, it felt oddly empty in a way I'd never experienced before. A sense of dread hung heavy. Looking at Marcus, his face said it all. Frowning, his preternatural eyes scanned everything.

Everything looked normal, but it didn't feel it. I rang her phone again and nothing. Pounding upstairs to see if she was hurt, but she wasn't there. As I walked into her bedroom, dizziness overcame me and I reached out to the wall to keep my balance. Blinking fast, my body went colder still, my vision blurred and I stumbled towards the bed to sit down, and a *presence*, like a soft blanket wrapped around me.

As I sat, I heard a cracking and something beneath me splintered. Pulling it out, it was an old hand mirror, oval with a long ornate handle. It was white with tiny faded red roses and gilded on the edge with gold. I'd never seen this before. What was odd was that the glass was dark, like obsidian. It looked like an antique. I stared into it, my dizziness subsiding and vision clearing, but all I saw was my reflection, cloudy in the dark mirror.

As Marcus came in I handed it to him. "What do you make of this? I've never seen it. Why is the glass dark?"

He paused as if looking for the words. "Ah, this is no ordinary mirror." Placing it down carefully, he said, "You won't find her here. This is a mirror used for portals. She's in a portal, somewhere." He looked a bit white, his face unchanged, wide eyed and shaking his head.

"What, a portal in space? Seriously? What does that even mean?" My body tightened. I knew he was withholding something. I guessed Lucius had taken her. Panic and a light sweat broke over me. How could I find her, help her? How do I get in there? Picking up the mirror, I looked dumbfounded at it.

"You can't. Even I can't. It's an old magic far stronger than myself. And that could be the entrance to many portals. She could be anywhere. One thing's for sure, Lucius won't harm her. If he's taken her, then he's serious about her. Demons don't take those they've little interest in into their secret places. No doubt she is well. She may not be happy, but she'll be safe at least. And don't bother searching the internet for portals. You'll get a ton of information, but you won't get anything useful. Real magic is protected. They don't put it out for just anyone to find."

"Have you ever been into a portal? What are they like?"

"No, I haven't. It's beyond my knowledge. I've never heard of a nephilim that can do portal magic. The others may know more. You must be strong and know she'll be alright. As I said, if he felt nothing for her, he wouldn't have taken her through one. As for that..." He pointed to the mirror. "That is a gateway. You could bring it; Acacius might know more. But when they return they may come through it. I don't think it being cracked will hinder that, but I'm not sure. I can feel the magic in here; it still feels active."

I felt deflated, I'd failed her. My selfishness had failed her, again. If I hadn't left, if only I'd been here.

Marcus interrupted my thoughts, "You couldn't have helped. You can't change what you don't understand."

I needed to be alone. I hugged the mirror to my chest and slowly rose from the bed. I followed Marcus out the door and down the stairs. We left to head home and I went back to my flat, and despite what Marcus said I did research portals. And what I did find, although not helpful for finding her, was disturbing.

I could use a mobile phone to open one. But none of the information was leading me to find her. The thought that I may never see her again made me sick. Anger boiled inside of me. Anger at myself for putting Nathaniel before her and livid at Lucius for taking her.

This supernatural world was more perilous to immortals than to mortals. I had made a mistake changing her. Had I left her mortal maybe she would have survived, but now... A bloody sweat broke over me and my heart wanted to stop beating. I knew it was futile but I kept thinking, *if only I'd left her mortal.*

My mind ran over and over this, but eventually I fell into a restless sleep as I sat on my bed staring into nothing.

I dreamt he had changed her into some hideous creature. Pure white face, taut skin with black holes for eyes, and a mouth like a large circle, screaming relentlessly. A thing, a thing without a soul like a zombie.

When I woke I was wet with sweat and breathing hard. Catching my breath, I lay there and welcomed the daylight that poured through my window. Rainbow hues splattered across the room, sunlight mixed with the light rain that fell.

My mind was confused with vivid dreams but when I woke up I had the sense of relief that what I had seen, was a dream. Then and there I vowed to find her. I would never leave her again. I had to remember I was not the same creature myself now.

I looked at the mirror beside my bed. Maybe I could use my instinct to enter it. Maybe not. I tried to ascertain some semblance, to feel her through the glass in whatever place she was now. As I closed my eyes and concentrated on her beauty, her laughter, her kindness and the soul I loved, I remembered something that had eluded me; The bad feeling I had before she had gone—what was that? I sat up and thought about those feelings I'd been getting.

Colours streamed through the windows as the sun outside caught the splinters of rain and cast rainbow shadows across the room. I spied tiny white orbs out of the corner of my eye, but when I looked they were gone. I must be tired still. But they started to flicker more, and one appeared in a burst in front of me. Once, twice. It seemed to be growing bigger. I rubbed my eyes, but again it appeared. I longed to be at Marcus's island right now. Just away from all this paranormal craziness. I'd go back to sleep but after that nightmare, that was shot. I lay down anyway. *Go away!*

Why did Marcus have to do that? Why did he have to drain that vampire?

"Marcus has always been wayward. We warned them to keep an eye on him, but they didn't listen and now every creature in Hell is loose in your tiny city, and we have to help clear up his mess. He should be killed."

I looked up as this unfamiliar, strained, high pitched voice came from seemingly nowhere. Maybe it was my subconscious. Maybe I *had* gone insane.

The orb was there, flickering, bigger, brighter. The tiniest face appeared suddenly, as white as snow with small dark eyes, quite nondescript except its eyelashes were so long and white they protruded right out. It looked androgynous whatever it was. It also felt noxious. It disappeared as quickly as it appeared. What the hell was that? I actually rolled over and buried my head in my pillow. No more! Then a thought came to me. *Maybe it could tell me where she is.* I sat up and waited. And waited. Again, the burst of light, like a cloudy bubble appeared and before the tiny face could speak, I asked, "Where's Rachel? Can you help me find her?"

The thing stared right into my eyes and it drew up closer. It laughed and disappeared. I needed to speak to Acacius and Halina. I knew they would know what this was. I didn't think I'd tell Marcus though; I'd need to keep those thoughts out of my mind for the time being.

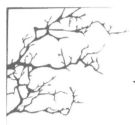

Vengeance

Anthony

IN THE TINY CITY OF Bath, I was surprised so many nephilim came to gorge themselves on the few vampires that had escaped discovery. There were many of these and unsurprisingly many vampires sought neighbouring cities and towns to escape the ravages of these beasts. But some of them actually sought each other out... I wondered why at first, why would a vampire willingly allow a nephilim to drink from it, but the thought occurred to me that when an act is most deviant, and once that thought is planted in the mind, then it grows and becomes alluring and even the strongest must succumb to its sin. Many will fall when temptation calls, and the consequences aren't thought of until it is too late. I knew this from experience but now as I watched, nephilim and vampire were pairing up.

With no Elite to govern them, though Nathaniel had amusingly wanted to allocate this role to himself and failed, this odd union became more prevalent. They were out together, mostly in small groups and the changes in the nephilim, their appearance was exotically different from when they arrived and they all now started hunting together.

128

Crime dropped in the city as a result and I saw for myself the newspaper reports of this inexplicable behaviour. Inexplicable to the mortals any way.

The mortal criminals started staying away from the parks, but that was futile as the fallen angels could now detect them by scent and hear their wicked thoughts from a distance with the dark blood that mixed in their bodies. It still haunted me that they said that blood contained the souls of man. I had drunk a lot and I tried many times to rationalise this.

I had to look harder to hunt. I started to seek out those corrupt people hiding their diabolical crimes in their homes and I broke the rule of not entering their homes.

My anger was especially petulant as I was powerless to find Rachel. I wanted revenge and I wanted her sweet scent and loving self wrapped in my arms. My stupidity of my past behaviour filled me with rage. How could so much go wrong so fast?

As I walked through the back streets of Bath's housing estates, I came across a small wiry man with such a stench of evil and hatred so strong that I gasped and put my hand to cover my nose. I immediately wanted to kill him.

Understand that as an immortal my senses are so honed that even the most seemingly normal of people, however fine they may seem to you, if they have a secret evil and debased life, we immortals *will* know it. We smell it, feel it, or hear it. Some humans have a keen sixth sense but as a vampire, it is ten times that. So I followed him which led me to his home on the outskirts of a poorer side of the city and there I saw for myself his evil lair.

A wife, two small children in the home, and dogs tied up outside. The house was on an estate and it was shoddy to look at. As his threatening presence entered the home, I heard the anger, the shouts and I spied on this little family—the children and mother in terror of this pathetic coward. Crouching down by the dogs, I spoke tenderly to them and stroked them. He had obviously taken his fear, his hatred out on these poor creatures, too.

Contrary to your popular myths, animals do not fear us as we do not and cannot drink their blood. Only yours. I untied the dogs from their cruel chains and let them out of the yard. Rachel and I always had an affinity for animals and this was not lost on me now.

Next I went to the metal dustbin in the corner of the small and filthy backyard. With the dogs out of the way, I picked up the metallic lid and dropped it on the floor. It made a loud clang against the yard floor, I then replaced it and sat on it, my head bowed like a little elf. I wanted to look as meek as possible.

The *mouth,* as I had aptly named it, came out and took the bait. I wasn't listening to it as it strolled over with its idiotic confidence and I slowly looked up at it, its rage and noise, inconsequential to life.

Slowly I stood up and smiled, my mouth curling, snarling, revealing my fangs. I am not tall but he was shorter and I spoke slowly, drawing out the words. "You are life's obscenity." And I bit his foul neck hard, sharp to impose pain, lingering, and drew on his blood slowly. He made a pathetic whimper and there I stayed, deliberately slow to draw out his death, his pain for as long as humanly possible. What was hardest for me was seeing his life. When I take blood I feel their emotions, sometimes see the lives my victims have led in a flash of images, not unlike a dream when sleeping. Abhorrent. Finally, I'd killed it and I dropped its body where I stood. I went to the window, staying in the shadows but called to the mother. "You are safe now; you are always watched now, protected. You never heard me." I turned and fled, carrying the pathetic body.

It is so simple. I found a construction site and buried it. Gone. I'm still hungry and the world is full of vicious criminals just waiting for me to end their pointless existence.

What I had done was highly forbidden, but who cared? I figured I could feed and people could be safe, the sick bastards deserved no justice, just as they had given none to any other. I hadn't felt righteous for a long time, but now this power felt good. And amongst so much chaos, who would know or care?

I knew my nephilim friends wouldn't agree, but Emidius had chosen me to do the dirty work she could not. She controlled the immortals; my job was to rid the place of the delinquents. I remembered she had told me not to kill, but I beg to differ.

In my new found sureness I wandered back into the city and came across a group of nephilim and vampires doing what I had just done. They were bleeding some vile excuse of a human when they spotted me. One of them, dark and lean, his large black feathered wings beating slowly, strode over to me, confident in his stride, his statuesque face perfectly unanimated, stern. "You are Anthony? I am pleased to meet you. I am Simon, this is Jonathan, and the vampire is Keera. We were just sorting the trash; she was hungry!"

I nodded and reined in my thoughts. I didn't care. "It was good to meet you," I said politely but walking away.

"Wait!"

Swiftly, I turned on my heels to face this being, full of blood and righteousness. "No! You may not take my blood. Don't try. You will regret it." I walked on calmly, without looking back, but the fool wouldn't take the hint.

"I'm sorry; I don't think I heard you right," he said. He leapt towards me, not taking no for an answer. But before he could continue, I did something so vile, so out of character I shocked and repulsed myself.

As he approached me, and I didn't need to read his mind to know that he assumed he *would* take my blood, I reached out and snapped his neck. I had no idea how I did this. I had no idea I could.

He crumbled to the ground and the other nephilim and vampire gasped in disbelief. I straightened my stance, looked them in the eyes, daring them to try, but they made no move towards me, until I turned around. The other nephilim rushed me. I turned and in an instant I sank my already-bloody fangs into his neck. He fought, trying to push me away and he was strong but the harder he pushed, the more angrily I sucked harder, faster and grabbed his hands. His wings beat violently, whacking my back, the pain terrible but exciting as I stole his soul, his life. I dropped him, delivering him to his God, should he be accepted now that he had fallen so far from favour. Their bodies burned fast and hot, as I had witnessed before.

My face was grim under the flashes of fire, and I eyed the woman and took a step towards her. She fled leaving her human victim somewhere between life and death. Not being completely stupid, I went over the mortal and surveyed him, I wanted to seek out his crime. A shallow despair swept over his face as he lay paralysed by her venom, conscious but unable to move. His crime was bad indeed and already satiated by blood, I snapped his neck. I grabbed up the body, just like my first kill so very long ago now, and dumped it in a fresh grave on the outskirts of the city. I was covered in dirt, having had to dig with my hands, and I felt sick at my unyielding punishment of others. But the power, the mercilessness felt good. I felt like a dark god who wanted revenge.

After my bloody activity, and caked in dirt, I wandered slowly back to my flat. Acacius had said, "How will this end?" and I wondered about that now. Would we destroy ourselves? As I was deep in thought, I ran into them—Marcus, Acacius, Halina, and my big-mouthed friend, Aaron.

Acknowledging each other only with nods, we stood watching as the scene of the two species played out in front of us. And so our vampire blood turned out to be infectious as the nephilim flocked to join in this forbidden activity. Unfortunately for the vampires and the nephilim alike.

The blood debasing their fair bodies, sending the once angelic descendants into a fraught spasm of violent changes. To see it was to believe it, the once beautiful white winged creatures of God's grace altered into shadowy beauties, dark wings, and fair skin tinted dark like obsidian shining under the moon's rays. Their grey eyes now black like their intentions, and their passion rife.

A handful went berserk. Observing from a distance under the watchful and intrigued gaze of Aaron, Halina, Marcus, and Acacius these few had to be stopped. It was harder for Acacius and his friends as they had rarely had to fight other of their kind, but as Aaron bluntly put it, from time to time small groups of his kin went wild and it was up to some of their order to gain control and rid the Earth of these delinquents.

"It is always the hardest, killing one's kin. And I mean both physically and emotionally. They match our strength, speed, and cunning and it fills our hearts with sorrow to cast them off. God alone knows their fate on death." Aaron's words were exacting and his tone quiet. It was a stark contrast to see Aaron so worried, he was usually mischievous and brusque.

"I am not happy to kill nephilim to save vampires. I cannot justify it," Halina spat. "I see the error of their ways, but my life has been spent doing the opposite. Anthony, you must leave us. What we have to do here will be unbearable for you to see, to watch. And..." she paused. "And after this night our association with you should be severed for your sake and the sake of Rachel. If vampires knew—and they will—that you stood by and watched us destroy your kin, you would both be hunted. Powerful as you are, you cannot withstand an attack from a thousand vampires. And they will never rest until you, Rachel, and no doubt all your human family and friends are dead. You must leave."

A cold sweat broke out over me as the realisation of her words filled my mind. Acacius and Marcus turned to me. They looked reluctant. We had only known each other for a short time but we had become fast friends. I felt sick in my gut with the thought of losing their friendship.

"No! There has to be another way. There is always another way!" Before they could act, I was walking towards the small band of violent angels. Marcus and Acacius stepped up to join me, but I was out ahead.

This group turned to watch me, eyeing me with evil intent and sniggers broke over their faces.

"Who the hell are you?" He was, as they all are, very, very tall, his fair hair now darkened and his skin glistening with fresh blood. He had gorged himself and the evidence of his savage change was still upon him. Blood and dirt covered his face, his clothes and his face grimaced like a gargoyle. The others looked as bad, they stank, and I was afraid but intent on ending this.

The vampires looked wasted. They were strewn around the side street that we had found this small gang in. Two looked exsanguinated, their crumpled bodies left in the gutter barely recognisable. The other two were barely alive and my instinct was to help them, my kin, though I didn't know them.

I looked the vile nephilim leader in the eye, but kept my distance due to his stench and blood-encrusted body. Holding myself tall, I spoke loudly, "I am Anthony and I am unlike any vampire you have known. These are my friends, my *nephilim* friends."

He sniggered and stepped forward, "Anthony, oh yes, we have all heard of *you*. The vampire saved by the demi-god. Your blood must taste sweet." He couldn't resist licking his lips. "But I have never heard of vampires and nephilim being friends." He sneered again. "But I suppose they like your blood."

"Quiet! I am Acacius and I cast judgement on you and your filth. You dishonour my race with your barbarism." Acacius rushed forward, startling me. His face was a torrent of anger, his soft features contorted with rage, blood rushing to his pale cheeks. His kin were motionless in their expression, their faces looked like statues. In unison, they stepped forward to join him, drawing their swords. That swift shrill sound of metal, as blades were drawn from their scabbards, long and slightly curved and so sharp that they sung.

Before the rabble could react, Halina, Aaron, Marcus, and Acacius had moved in like wolves onto prey and felled the heads of these berserkers in lightning speed. Their blood spurted fast and then in a flash their bodies ignited that blue-white flame and they were no more. In shock I ran to the vampires who were barely conscious.

I could hear the disapproval of Halina as I assessed which vampire to help first. Two young male vampires looked out of place, out of time. Their curly locks and boyish faces looked out of place, too innocent to be so ferociously attacked. Black with bruises, bitten and bloody. I bit my wrist and held it over the smallest one, he didn't look older than fourteen, and his brethren only a few years older. They must be brothers, they were so similar. As he started taking my blood, I assessed the other, who was now hardly breathing. Rasping sounds came faintly from him and my heart bled that these boys had been turned so young and now their dark existence almost stolen from them.

Aaron came on his own, sheathing his sword, and moving swiftly to set the other vampire next to me. He stood for a moment and looked down, his red hair masking his eyes, but he was smirking with such a large inhuman grin. I nodded and bit my other wrist. And so I had two vampires, one on each wrist, each hardly alive but drinking my blood to bring them back into our shadow existence.

Halina looked me over, lips pursed and eyes small, shaking her head in disgust before leaving.

Marcus, Acacius, and Aaron stayed with me, fascinated it seemed by what they were watching. Never before had nephilim helped vampire, nor watched as these two immortals started to regain life. My strong blood invigorated them and slowly their appearance started to change and their bruises faded, growing fainter. We were unaware of the noise from the streets. Silence gripped us as we waited patiently for the brothers to come around. Marcus knelt beside me, perched in wonder.

Something had changed this night, something profound. The old rules had been broken. I no longer cared what others thought of me, I could only act in the way I saw best whether right or wrong. I had changed and I would never have thought that my actions would lead to such a shift in power between supernatural species.

We were now the outlaws, acting against laws and traditions dating back thousands of years. We were fast kin and I felt excited. I felt like I had a purpose, to help regardless of species.

The boys, I couldn't think of them as anything else, no matter how long they'd been vampire, shifted back on their legs and hands backing against the wall, confused and scared by the scene in front of them. A vampire who had saved their life, but surrounded by nephilim.

The older one went to speak, but shock held his tongue and his eyes were wide with disbelief.

"It's okay, you're safe now. The others who attacked you, they're gone. These nephilim killed them and won't harm you. I gave you my blood. I am sorry about your friends, we arrived too late." I spoke gently, but they were clearly afraid. "I am Anthony. And these are my friends. Yes, nephilim, but not like the ones who attacked you."

As I stood and turned to leave, the youngest spoke quietly. "Why, why did they save us?"

Now Acacius spoke, though he didn't move. His voice, so deep and booming, despite his attempt to reassure, echoed around the small side street. "Those nephilim were an abomination to our kind. I see that some have taken to drinking the blood of your kind and while I do not condemn them for this practise I will not tolerate cruelty. It sickens me. It is Anthony here that saved your lives, for in truth without him, we would not have saved yours.

"Do not speak of this to anybody and make sure the blood you consume comes from criminals and degenerates. I am sure you will follow these instructions, as you would, no doubt, rather have us as friends than enemies?" Acacius smiled and his face returned to his smooth angelic looks.

They both nodded and we smiled and left them to contemplate their most bizarre night. We strode through the tiny city. The angels hid their swords beneath their long flowing black coats, except Aaron who wore a red velvet coat to match his hair. Without discussing it before, we knew we would patrol the city in case there were any more berserk nephilim. We attracted a lot of attention and as we walked a group of plump, drunk human men started heckling us.

Something caught my eye in that dreary damp evening, I caught a flash of something, and heard an unearthly growling. Before I realised it, I was running towards it and found myself standing at an iron fence surrounding a park, looking in. It was dimly lit with only a few street lamps and the rich smelling foliage.

I heard the noise again. Scrambled sounds of not one being but two, maybe three. Acacius had joined me at the gate, along with Aaron and Marcus. And then the beast stood up, a colossus of a nephilim. Blood glistened on his face under the lamp light and he eyed us with indifference and then returned to his blood bath.

"Anthony!" A shrill, weak sound came from behind this beast.

A sudden sweat broke out on me and fear seized my body as I recognised that weak voice. It was so sudden with no time to think.

"Nicolas!" Anger and fear gripped me suddenly. I started looking for ways to breach the giant.

"Who is Nicolas?" Aaron barked at the sudden awareness that the situation had suddenly turned worse. It was now personal.

"Tyrell, the Elite despot Jamie killed, Tyrell held Nicolas in servitude against his will. He is a good man." But before I finished I was already half way across the park heading towards this brute to save my friend.

The colossus turned and straightened up, his massive structure intimidating and muscular. He looked like a Titan. His voice boomed and echoed so deep I could feel the ground reverberating. "Welcome." His eyes cast over our little group. He eyed me, his huge mouth salivating blood. "Good, let me show you your true fate. I will end your suffering; take you to a dark solitude for all eternity. Ah, I smell her blood in you, Anthony...good."

His large eyes surveyed behind me, and his face grew animated by what he saw. Then he laughed, deeply, his voice echoed. "You cannot harm me, boy. I have lived for thousands of years and killed thousands of your kind, but try, please. It will be interesting to play before I drain you of her precious blood. I knew he would bring me some good fortune." He signalled to Nicolas who was dying, crumpled on the floor behind this fiend.

Acacius, Aaron, and Marcus had joined me in the park, keeping their swords hidden for the moment no doubt to gain the element of surprise.

Charging forward with all the courage I could muster, I leapt at his neck. I didn't reach it as he caught me mid-air, his huge arms like thick branches, and I struggled like a cat, writhing and contorting myself, snapping at his neck.

Marcus lost no time and ran behind him, slashing at his back. The monster tossed me away easily. As I thudded to the ground and looked up, I saw Acacius and Aaron hacking at the monster, their swords so sharp he was being sliced to ribbons. My friends spun around the giant nephilim, stabbing and slicing at every opportunity. Being smaller has its advantages.

Their speed was astonishing. The giant roared, trying to frighten and distract, but he couldn't grab their swords. They were just too fast and sharp. Blood bath is a word I could use to describe the scene before me. His arms and back were ripped and bleeding from their cutting swords. Aaron darted under the nephilim's swinging arm, dodging the fist attached to the arm. Seeing his opportunity to weaken the monster further, he hacked off his right hand. The monster's scream was deafening.

As he doubled in pain, protecting the severed stump, Marcus swung his mighty sword twice, taking off his head.

In the carnage I had forgotten about Nicolas until I heard his whimper. Getting up from where I had been thrown, I conquered my pain and sought out Nicolas. I walked tentatively around the carcass and quickly pulled Nicolas away, knowing what would follow. I just managed to get Nicolas away from the nephilim beast, when the monster flashed that brilliant blue-white flame and was gone. The smell was rancid.

I fed Nicolas, holding him up against my chest as he drank. I didn't know if he'd survive even with my blood. He had been ravaged beyond any I'd saved, except Nathaniel. I could barely recognize him. But he drank and grew stronger. As his frantic sucking slowed, I was aware that dawn was coming. He got up and turned my way, nodding his thanks and walked slowly away. No words were needed. He hadn't really been a friend, more of an acquaintance, but I knew, I could sense from him, that he never wanted to do the wrong thing. He'd always just been in the wrong place at the wrong time or manipulated and used.

Sometimes we are thrown into circumstances so beyond our control that all we can do is make the best of them until we have a chance to change. Our chance to be free and live our lives by our own choosing. I hoped I wasn't wrong about Nicolas. If I was, and he really was evil, I would kill him. But at least he was given the chance.

I waited another moment, watching Nicolas fade into the dark. Aaron and Acacius had left moments before, and were already out of sight, having taken to the skies on their massive wings. I shook myself from my thoughts and scurried away from where I'd been sitting with Nicolas, my head dizzy with the sudden movement after losing so much of my own blood. Marcus, seeing my weakness, grabbed me around the waist and unfurled his wings, sending us into the lightening sky. I tensed and held my breath, vertigo becoming worse.

Marcus laughed and shouted over the wind, "Breathe, Anthony, we're not going far!"

We were on the other side of the city in seconds and I felt breathless, never having experienced flying like that before.

Through Anthony's Eyes

Anthony

THEY WERE STRIKING and projected energy of power that made mortals stare in wonder. They looked beautifully deadly.

Marcus could have never have foreseen such events unfolding on that fateful night when he bit the vampire, but now the consequences of his action, leading to more nephilim plunging into darkness had unleashed a malevolent power.

The balance of good and evil had shifted, and as the nephilim paired with vampires and lost their piety, so, too, did the veil of reality open further, and the onslaught of those from the underworld flooded in. And as these fiends came into mortal reality, the effect on man increased.

Their anger, hate, fear—call it what you will—manifested further feeding on the malicious energy. And the fallen angels, try as they might, were unable to fight this malignant power, having succumbed to a dark energy themselves. The tiny city filled with thick smog, the haze of the sinister world with these things pouring through.

As I walked through the city centre the people had a grey pallor in their faces. It was startling to see so many almost hunched, dreary looking, washed-out and all the while apparitions loomed and hovered over them, following them like a ball and chain.

A fog descended over Bath like a heavy blanket, encasing all within it, oppressive and severe. It lasted for days and I noted the news and scientists struggling for an explanation, telling people it was a chemical haze due to a leak in a nearby industrial plant. People were warned to stay indoors, but as these mortals were so intoxicated with doom, they didn't heed the warnings. Of course, it wasn't a chemical leak; it was the descent of abominable entities spilling forth.

Men's souls were bleeding, bleeding with sickness and fear. And as this gloom lasted, it of course attracted more of its kind. The city of Bath became a haven to the undead. Demons, vampires, werewolves, and ghouls all converging and looking to steal the spirit of mortal flesh.

Some wanted the souls of the living to make themselves physical, others were just angry. Furious at the weak mortal flesh that had, until now, dominated their existence.

A feast of blood and souls, easy pickings for those from the shadows, ready to drag away the empty soulless beings into the abyss. The helpless humans, unable and unwilling to see what was happening around them, blinded themselves to the darkness and left as hollow, empty carcasses.

I was unable to stand by and watch this without doing something, but what could I do?

Acacius, Halina, and Aaron were called upon as they had abstained from drinking the vampire blood. Acacius and his kin, always ready for battle were now growing weary with so many breaking through the veil.

"Anthony, Nathaniel, we need a new plan. And you need to help! I won't lie to you, I have never known of vampires fighting demons or ghouls, and I have never known of vampires succeeding in doing so. I don't even know if you can help. *But* the veil has broken as you see, and these fiends created by man are becoming too many. I could call upon more of my kin, the untouched ones to come here, and they would. They could arrive swiftly, and I am contemplating this seriously. But you, Marcus, and all vampires and fallen nephilim would be slaughtered by them. They would show you no mercy."

Acacius continued, "So either we hatch a plan to destroy these phantoms of fear, or I shall have no other choice. I will not stand by and watch as humans are consumed by their own fear, their own hate. I'm eager to hear your thoughts."

I understood completely Acacius's concerns and I wished the others could come, but without killing me and mine. "There has to be some connection. I mean I have the blood of a demi-god within me. Surely that counts for something. Do you think maybe she knew this would happen?"

For once, Nathaniel was serious and listened whilst Acacius and I talked, as did the others. I knew I was stronger now, not just physically but emotionally. I felt ready, ready to act, that I did have some higher purpose other than bleeding people.

"You're right, yes, that has to be the key. Marcus, you, too, have her blood after drinking from Anthony. As does Nathaniel. We need to plan, and fight back."

I felt lifted somehow, like I was aiming for a higher purpose and this was what Acacius had told me. I was transcending from the mundane existence which most creatures, preternatural or not, live in. Like Acacius, my ideas, beliefs, my principles were aiming higher. I had never felt this before. I had acted without self interest in the past to be sure when Jamie and I had sought out to destroy the Elite butchers, but this was different. I have to admit, most humans may not live on a high level. That is, most people are concerned with being comfortable rather than making sweeping changes and acting for others. But still, their souls were at stake. Even Nathaniel was enthused, as I read his emotions I think it was for the right reasons as opposed to the excitement. I wasn't enthusiastic having Nathaniel there, but we needed all the help we could get. An eternity to be angry is a long time.

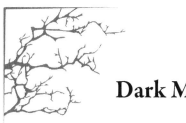

Dark Mirrors

Anthony

I WENT TO RACHEL'S empty home and walked slowly upstairs, sat on her bed and picked up the dark mirror. In the research it said you could use mobile phones, something to do with the frequencies, I didn't really know what I was doing but I was damned if I was going to leave her where ever the hell she was with that demon. A demon who wanted to mate with her!

And I concentrated. I'd charged her phone when I was last there and I hoped, prayed that it could help link me to her now. What I'd found on the the web was sketchy and full of sinister tales. But for Rachel, I was willing to try anything.

Her room still had an unease about it, the energy filled me, pushed against me. It was like I wasn't alone. My body was colder than usual and strange prickling sensations tingled on my head and arms, as if I was being prodded by some unseen force. But I had to find her. I texted Marcus to tell him what I was doing so that at least someone would know if I got lost.

Immediately, I got a text back saying he was on his way and not to do anything. His text message shouted at me as he'd capped all the letters. Still, I sat there, grasping the mirror in my hands. Stillness. Then thoughts came into my mind—relax.

It was like a light bulb moment. I decided to stand up. When I had learnt Kung Fu and Qi Gong in my human life I was taught techniques about chi-energy that most people do not. I also remembered that I needed some respect in what I was doing and must ask permission to enter the portal where Rachel was. I learned *that* from YouTube, and was following all the information I had. All portals have Guardians. All though what that really meant I had no idea, it's just what I read.

Quietening my restless mind, I took some deep breaths then started moulding the energy around me by making what we call in Qi Gong an energy ball. I felt immediately calm and centred and the energy ball started to build up fast. I focused my intention on the mirror in front of me that was now laying on the bed. As I did this a breeze brushed past me, but I didn't stop. I didn't stop as Marcus flew into the room to grab me, and then I was gone.

All I felt next was being pulled into a vortex, rushing fast downwards with streams of rainbow-coloured lights pulsating around me, bright and so beautiful. My stomach flipped and I remember thinking, *don't forget to breathe* as I was caught up in the experience. Air whirled past me and the lights flashed, hypnotising me.

I was aware that Marcus was beside me. Disorientated and on my back, instinct to hold my head which pounded in pain. Cold bit at my fingers fiercely, and looking down I saw that I was sat in snow my other hand steadying me and wet with ice.

Marcus was beside me, and also rubbing his head, sitting up, crouching forward. He shook himself, blinking.

I looked around me and the surroundings were a forest in winter. Most trees were bare and thick snow and ice covered them and as far as I could see.

Marcus made no sound as he studied this. His face said it all. Angry but also fascinated and afraid. His lips tight, eyes squinting through that brilliant bright light.

I remembered then what he had said, that no nephilim had entered a portal. His adventurous spirit made him an excellent companion. Not only had he been the first of his kind to drink vampire blood, he was now the first of his kind to cross through a portal. I couldn't help it, but this thought and the shock of what was happening made me sputter out a laugh.

He narrowed his eyes and nodded slightly at my thoughts while extending his arm to help me up. It was bitter cold and the realisation slowly dawned on me, that as well as finding Rachel, I also had to find a way home. I didn't have the mirror, that was on the bed, but I did have the phones. Hopefully that would be enough.

As I pulled them out of my pocket, my heart sank. Staring at the phones, I saw that they were warped, the casings slightly twisted. And dead.

Startled by rustling in the tree tops, I looked up. I thought I saw birds flying off due to our presence, but looking again they were dark diaphanous shapes of birds. Not actual birds, grey shadows, their cries silent in that wintry place.

I took a deep breath and tried to relax. Hoar frost on the leaves and vegetation had left tiny spikes of frozen ice, like thick needles of sparkling glass. Bitter, the cold was already starting to bite me and my emotions felt suddenly melancholy. A severe beauty encased this landscape, brutal in its extreme. The light from the sky and glowing around the trees was glacial blue and this was daylight. How cold would night time be?

"So, my clumsy friend, what now?" were the first words from Marcus. "I hope you know a way back or we might both die frozen to death. She won't be here. A demon wouldn't go somewhere so cold; they don't like it. They prefer somewhere hot." He didn't look at me as he spoke, but looked around for some clue as to what to do, where to go.

"That was your choice to follow me, but I am glad you're here. I need to concentrate on relaxing my mind. I'm confident I'll get a sign, an instinct or intuition."

Shaking his head, he was clearly pissed off and didn't bother to answer. His face was stern and frowning, lips pursed, and his body was rigid with anger.

I shoved my hands in pockets, regretting not being more prepared and wearing a coat. Thank God I had a jumper on. I relaxed and breathed deeply. Nothing. As I did, all I was aware of was how cold I was feeling. My hands were like ice and my toes were losing feeling. Breathing the air in was chilling my body, my insides, and the light was blindingly bright. I found it hard to focus on anything else.

The light started to fade fast, the shapes and the trees of the forest turned from that glacial blue to black. I was glad I had vampire vision to see, or more aptly stumble through that forest. I stopped. My heart raced as I saw a figure in the distance against a tree, and Marcus upon reading my mind stopped dead.

But looking again it was just the shadow of a tree casting the shape of a human figure. I breathed deeply and continued on. It was so eerie. No sounds at all except the clumping and crunching of our feet on that deep snow and now my feet felt like blocks of ice.

In my mind's eye I saw creatures here, human-like but moving swiftly like animals, on all fours, their back legs jointed like wolves. It was like they were composed of dark clouds. Fear started in me as I was uncertain this was a vision. I looked over at Marcus for reassurance.

He seemed to shimmer into a diaphanous form of himself, his face weary which was disconcerting as he is always so robust.

As the cold grew with my fear, I wanted more than ever the comfort of hot, sweet blood to warm me, to awaken my senses but I dared not dwell on this.

My instinct was to concentrate and keep walking, no talking and wander to the place. I knew on some level I would find something. I hurried my pace, careful not to say anything so as not only to appease my friend, but also to keep from disturbing whatever may be in this place.

As we walked on in that deep snow, the whole place had a deathly silence except for us. I wished we could move without sound, like the fanciful tales of vampires flying. And then fear grabbed me in the throat and stomach as my vision adjusted to the figures standing around us. Bipeds, but not human. Eerie by day, more so at night. There were a dozen of them. Marcus had seen them just before me and stood like stone, hardly daring to breathe. Should I speak? Should I run? I could fight but I knew I was outnumbered. Better to speak, then run... Thoughts and fear filled me fast.

They moved towards us slowly, encircling us.

Speak, I told myself. It was hard to speak when your throat turned to sawdust. Swallowing hard, I tried to sound confident. "I am Anthony. I have come here looking for my friend."

They growled, slowly edging towards us, their eyes like scarlet dots in the night.

"We mean you no harm. Have you seen another vampire and a demon?"

At these words they stopped, and not one moved. I thought, *if they are transparent, how can they hurt us? Can their condition affect us?* Looking down at my arms, my legs, I still looked solid.

"Who are you?" I murmured.

"No one has entered here. No one. You must leave or die." The one that spoke, obviously the largest creature, appeared part human, part wolf. He was maybe seven, eight feet high. Though slightly transparent, his presence was terrifying. An animal-human hybrid with the advantage of the wolf's muscular limbs. His face contorted in a mixture of wolf/ human, threatening just to look at. And his voice sounded deeper and more ethereal than the nephilim.

"How did you get here?"

Anthony, shut the hell up! Marcus's thoughts flew into my mind urgently.

Again, low growling. A face off. I was freezing and too scared in all honesty to fight, and how would I fight something not physical? Maybe they would infect us to become like them.

"No demons would dare to enter here," a resounding bellow came. They moved to leave a gap in their circle so that we could pass through. We struggled not to look back as we walked through.

They followed us at a distance for a while and neither of us spoke. We communicated through our minds only, which seemed unnatural but not as unnatural as that experience. Mile after mile we trudged, and all feeling in my body had left long ago. Our breathing sounded so loud, I heard my heart pumping at times, and adrenaline pushed us forward. My mind kept playing tricks on me. *What if those creatures followed us? What if they bit me, became solid, and tore me to pieces! What if...*

"Shut the fuck up. Do you never stop with the thinking?" Marcus whispered. "If you don't stop, I'll drink your blood and leave you here with them. Okay!" As I looked at him in disbelief he was grinning widely, a little tear of laughter in his eye.

We came to a tiny waterfall, a clearing and here I felt that the energy had shifted. The slight light of the moon caught the water and I could see stones surrounding it. Tall stones of maybe a few feet high where the landscape changed.

One of the stones looked like an animal face and I knew this was a sign of a portal but something else nagged at me.

"Is this it?" Marcus whispered.

"Yes, but there's something else here. I feel it. Some sort of knowledge for me to know." I crouched down and closed my eyes, breathing in that clean crisp air. I'm not sure how long I was doing that but I felt a swishing and a whirling around me.

To my knowledge, Marcus didn't feel this sensation. Without questioning, I opened my eyes, got up slowly without knowing I was doing so and went to the side of the waterfall. Putting my hand behind it, I looked at Marcus and nodded my head for him to come.

With one hand holding onto him, I put the other behind the water and felt something like glass. The water was icy cold but this object was hot and the size of my hand. Pulling it out, I saw it was a clear crystal with flecks of gold inside and remarkably, a tiny blue flame. I gasped, seeing that flame, how was that possible? I didn't know what it was or what it meant, but within seconds we were hurtling through a whirlwind of energy, me still grasping tightly to Marcus and the stone. I felt dizzy again, disoriented as we seemed to be travelling through a tunnel again. Everything was whirling and rainbow lights flickered around us as before. I prayed in that instant that we would end up where we'd begun.

Breathe. I had to remember to breathe and as I opened my eyes we were back in Rachel's room looking at the dark mirror.

"Thank God," he panted and sat on the bed. "Whatever that is, you were meant to find it!" We both collapsed on the bed exhausted.

As we sat there I pulled out the crystal flame. It was hot and the blue flame flickered strongly and bright. I pulled him up by his shoulder. "Let's get out of here. I don't want to end up somewhere else. I don't feel safe in here!"

Nodding and moving quickly, he agreed. He looked normal now and we went downstairs to the living room and sprawled out on the sofa, so relieved to be back in our world. Warmer and where everything looked solid.

"If I hadn't had your blood in me I may not have survived that. I had the strangest sensation of disappearing!" he said quietly.

I threw my thoughts elsewhere. I didn't want him to know that he had been. Thank God it had been him with me, not Acacius! At least with my blood in Marcus, that had helped, I guessed.

"Next time you do something like that, don't take me!" He laughed, letting out all that fear, that anger.

I spluttered a laugh, too, the relief of all that anxiety, all that cold and those Hellish creatures. I still couldn't speak much. I was too in awe of the whole experience. I wanted to know, though, what the time was and hard though it was to pull my tired, heavy body off the sofa, I went to kitchen to look at Rachel's world clock. Four days! We'd been away four days! And still no Rachel. Despair would have gripped me, but I was too tired and shocked for it to get to me.

I went back in the living room and sat down, still clutching the crystal, and now I put it on a table. Quietly I told him, "We've been away for four days! But it felt like just a few hours."

"One very long freezing day. I told you, Anthony, portals are the strangest places."

"What do you suppose this fire crystal does?"

"Kill demons, I guess. You were obviously meant to have it and that's why you were allowed into the portal."

"Have you ever seen one before?"

"No, and I've never heard of one, but the others may have. Nephilim have been around a long time so I suspect Acacius or Halina might know something, even Aaron. Lucius would no doubt love to get his hands on it. You need to guard it well. Don't blab anything to Nathaniel either, that would be my advice! Keep it hidden for now. I can't even text them, my phone's melted just like yours."

I was weary and slowly warming up after the bone chilling cold of the realm beyond the portal. I wanted to go hunting, but my body aching and weak, I resigned myself to just staying put until I was rested and warmer.

After a night and a day of resting in Rachel's home with the heating on full and several hot showers, I felt ready to see Acacius. I wanted to go with Marcus since I was taking this strange crystal with me, so we headed to the North-East area of the city, where Acacius, Aaron, and Halina had rented a house. I didn't want to hunt until I had left it in their careful possession, and I hoped they could tell me something about it.

As we walked across the city that evening, the atmosphere hadn't changed from when we'd left and the mortals looked as gloomy and despondent as ever. Wraiths were thick and wailing, it disturbed my mind a lot as it did Marcus, and for a second I swear I saw him fade again.

Aaron was in the garden imparting divine energy on all the neighbourhood cats, dogs, and wildlife. An angelic Dr. Doolittle. Halina was on the Internet or the *Light web*, yes there is a hidden internet for immortals, their own encrypted version.

"You think because we're old we're computer illiterate?" Acacius laughed. "It's not only you vampires that have your own technology!" He was happy to see us, sighing then smiling he guided us into his home. "So, what happened to you two? We couldn't get hold of you and we picked up something had happened. Marcus, something has changed about you. I sense it."

Marcus looked at me to explain and sunk down into a chair seemingly exhausted, which was unusual for him.

"I opened a portal, we both went in, and I was led to this!" I blurted out, pulling out the fire crystal and laying it carefully on a table. Gasping, they all stopped, staring intently at it, moving towards it.

"Do you know what that is?" Halina asked me.

"Nope, I was hoping you would tell me. Marcus thinks it could help rid us of the wraiths and the demons."

"It will certainly do that and more," Halina whispered looking in awe of the crystal. She edged towards it, reaching out to touch it, but stopping just before her fingers reached it. It was as if it was the Holy Grail. "And you, *you* carried it?" she asked, her face frowning, voice confused.

"Yes!"

They looked at each other.

"C'mon, the suspense is killing me." I laughed.

"A fire crystal is a rare thing indeed, and there isn't much knowledge on them. Few have heard about them, even fewer have ever seen one. None from this dimension have ever seen one. You are right, you were led to this. These objects pick their owner. They are never found by accident. They contain massive power, a force to dispel and destroy evil. But you have to know how to wield them. We can help you and find some information on that."

"I, *we,* wanted to bring it here. We were concerned about others stealing it, misusing it. Can you help to keep it safe?"

"You were right to do that," Aaron interjected. "If this fell into the wrong hands, the consequences would be diabolical. Yes, we can definitely help." He turned to the others. "This will help enormously, but..." He looked at Marcus. "I fear for Marcus. I'm not sure how we can help you, I am so sorry to say. I know I speak bluntly but we all know it, you are fading into eternity. The blood was probably the first thing to start diminishing your life force and now you've entered a portal that has strained your life force even more. You need to write everything so we have a record. Maybe give us an idea how to save you. Maybe you could access your Akashic records for clues. I don't know, but although I have found this whole nephilim-vampire blood sharing fascinating, I had a deep suspicion that it would lead to the destruction of yourself and the vampires."

Marcus sat up. "I know. I don't want to die, but I've felt this way for a few days now. Like a weariness but... Don't blame yourself, Anthony, about the portal. I made this decision when I tasted her blood. In an instant I changed my fate, and even though now I sense it's leading to my end, my only regret is the consequences that have led to the veil opening and affecting humans. I would never have wanted that, and I will do everything to right that wrong. I intend to correct it at all cost to me. And then at least, I can pass away with peace."

We were all silent and sad. We knew he spoke the truth, in our hearts we knew. He was such a character he would leave a large void in our lives.

"Plus," Marcus continued. "No nephilim has entered a portal and though it was physically uncomfortable, I am glad I got to experience it. We saw the strangest things there. I don't regret that. My story might be different though had we not found a way out!"

Waxing Shadows

Rachel

IT WAS NICOLAS WHO found us. I hadn't seen Nicolas since Nathaniel held me captive at the Elite headquarters and after the Elite were wiped out. I'd assumed Nicolas had died alongside them.

Nicolas had been their assistant, merely a pawn for those in power to use, and it was suggested that his maker had turned him simply to do his bidding. Nicolas was not liked by his superiors because he had some semblance of a conscience. He was too weak and powerless to question them, but it was evident that he wasn't happy with the atrocities they performed. He was seen as feeble, but seeing him now in the park with these creatures I'd helped escape from the portal, was welcome relief.

And more so, he began to share his knowledge and helped us.

"Rachel! Thank the Gods, you're alive! I had no idea." His smile filled his face and I felt that he found great reassurance, as he had been alone and scared amongst this chaos. I couldn't blame him. Since I had been away, the situation had escalated and more deadly creatures roamed. I had taken the shadow people back to my tiny home. It was cramped and claustrophobic, and tonight we were going across the park towards Acacius' home. The shadow people stuck together in huddles as we crept towards the other side of the city, their eyes full of fear and flinching at every sound. Even the shadow birds above were silent. We had seen the entities oozing out of humans, the wails and screams piercing our ears, and the flashes here and there of green lights. Green flashes I now knew meant the presence of demons. No wonder they were scared of this dark twisted reality that I had brought them into.

Nicolas stopped short and looked at them in amazement and trepidation. And he looked long at me. I allowed him time for his assessment, interested in what advice or knowledge he could offer.

"Where have you all come from? In all my years I haven't seen a Shadow person. And you, Rachel? I sense a change in you. Something's different."

I smiled and nodded slightly.

"Where have you all come from? What has happened? Rachel, I feel an immense power coming from you." His shaky voice gave him away.

"Good to see you, Nicolas." I took a deep breath before relaying my misfortune. "I was kidnapped by a demon and taken to a portal, where I befriended these creatures who helped me escape." His face dropped, mouth open, aghast. "I killed the demon. And so here we are, and I know nothing of what to do next. We were in fact on our way to see Acacius."

Now he nodded and scratched his head, walking closer towards me and the shadow people, eyeing us as if we were some new unknown thing.

"How did you kill the demon? They are immensely hard to kill," he asked tentatively.

"I drank his blood, ripped out his heart, removed his head, and burnt the remains." I spoke so matter of fact that when I heard those words I myself was shocked that I had done this, but that now seemed an age ago.

His eyes were wide with astonishment. Looking from them to me he seemed too shocked for words. His words stumbled out, "You drank its blood? And yet you live? I never knew they even *had* blood..."

"He was physical. It wasn't like the blood of mortals, or vampires. I don't know what it will do in the long term. I feel very different and I felt a painful transformation after. But more from the light that emitted from him when I removed his head. Without that, without killing him, we would still be trapped, wherever we were. Nicolas, we need your help."

"Shadow people can fight demons, did you all know that?" he spoke directly to them. He continued, more animated in his new role of helper. "I had read in an old text a long time ago about this. As you have no physical substance, and demons once materialized take on physical form, it *is* possible to take their energy from them, to take it for yourselves. I believe you simply track them and merge into them, although—and this is the fatal bit—you have to do this when they are unawares."

"You mean we could become physical again?" one of them asked.

"Yes, but what happens after that, little is known. There is no other way that I know that you can become a physical manifestation."

"But wouldn't we become evil? Damned?" one of them asked.

Nicolas raised his eyebrows, as if trying to remember the text he had read so long ago. "Are you not damned now? Are we not all damned? Look at Rachel, the blood of demon in her. Have you become malicious, Rachel? I would consider that it has much to do with the individual. The energy of a demon is cruel, spiteful. Usually, because of their reliance on a mortal, they're full of anger over not being able to exist on their own terms. They can only exist once their victim acknowledges them, to become physical. Ah, but once that victim dies they go back to a nonphysical state and the whole process starts again.

"They are also hated, pretty much by everyone, mortal or otherwise. And their victims are mostly not evil, they are susceptible, naïve, but not evil. What *you* do with that power would be up to you."

"So, will you help us?" I asked him again.

He paused, looked at the shadow people and back to me. "Rachel, it would be a pleasure."

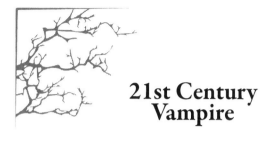

21st Century Vampire

Anthony

NATHANIEL AND I WENT out to the outskirts of the city to hunt, where the once seemingly grand Georgian building surround the city. Once these buildings held the upper classes of Bath, but now most were tiny flats with many people packed into them.

We climbed the walls of one of these buildings and sat at the top on the roof and waited. All we had to do was open our minds, our emotions, and we would sense where in the building the vile mortals were, and the type of maliciousness they were engaged in. We could smell it.

It felt better hunting like this, rather than just being out in the open.

This time, Nathaniel had a plan. Evil, it seems, attracts evil. His vampire friends had created an app that would hack and store information taken from our victim's hardware, hence why particularly that night, we were hunting victims in their own home. The details, Nathaniel wanted Darren to explain to me.

I was impressed with Nathaniel. He had not only come up with this plan, but with the help of others, they had started a database of vile criminals that was being shared throughout the paranormal world. I found it an amusing concept, almost like

163

ordering from a fast food place. I could go on line and pick who I wanted to eat! And since there were no rules since the demise of the Elite, technically we didn't have to keep them alive.

Mainly, the rule of not killing was imposed, not because of compassion but because getting rid of hundreds, if not thousands of bodies is far harder in the twenty-first century. Or so I've been told.

And so we sat and waited. Ridiculous how fast we felt their corrupt minds and emotions of those in that building, and the sheer amount of delinquents. Awareness of their cruel intentions, their self-loathing, their fear. So many in this building. They really do attract each other.

Nathaniel refused to do anything until he had text his other vampire friends so that we could all clear up that filth in one night. I'd never known he cared that much about humanity. I'd never known him to be so responsible.

"I hear you, Anthony. I am not the same vampire that I was when we first met. Being staked and set on fire changed me." He laughed sarcastically. "But really, with everything going on, I am livid with the amount of diseased sick mortals on the increase. So we got organised. We'll easily hack into their software and then Darren, who you'll meet, will upload all their details, their friends, family, contacts. If we discover any of these to be cruel, we'll add them to our list. The app Darren created gives you all their information. It's a new world my friend, and that means we no longer have to prowl the night like creatures from a bygone age. No, now we just go online. We have infiltrated their dark web with our own. *Our blood web.*"

Using human technology against humans, it was elegant and brilliant. A new age indeed. If we kept up like this, whatever they created we could use. No more hanging around dark, wet parks in the freezing cold waiting. I liked this idea much better; it was much more sophisticated.

I hadn't met his friends and it was amazing to see, one by one, all these vampires appear on the roof alongside us. The few that managed to escape the clutch of the nephilim.

Darren was the first to arrive. He was gracious and excited to be using the app he and his friends had developed. I didn't know how long he'd been immortal, but his manner was so gentlemanly that I guessed he wasn't of the twenty-first century. He was about my height, just under six-foot with short, blonde messy hair that he'd run some product through. Like most vampires, he was dressed in jeans, jumper and coat. It was cold tonight and we feel the cold more than humans. Gone are the archaic days of cloaks and top hats, although some wear modern clothes with antique accessories.

He showed me the tech on his phone and within twenty-minutes there was a dozen vampires with us, ranging in ages from when they'd been turned. Eight of them were female, quite a few were flamboyant. They did wear the more traditional vampire goth clothing, flowing coats, leather jeans. Nathaniel introduced us. Some were clearly loners. Their manner was reserved, indifferent. Others were eager to make my acquaintance, having heard about my adventures. Rob and Julian introduced themselves and their vampire partners, Louise and Alicia. They were richly dressed with tailored long coats. They were local. I was surprised at how many I'd never met.

And the vampire brothers who I and my nephilim friends had saved from the rogue nephilim, arrived. Their names were Johnathan and Patrick, and they looked well. We all chatted eagerly but quietly amongst ourselves, hidden from mortal view high up on that Georgian roof top.

"There are several entrances here," Nathaniel addressed everyone. "Once you're in and fed, look for their computers, phones, iPads or tablets. Hack everything. Take these."

Darren handed everyone a few different types of USB sticks. "Julian and I have put these together. Once you've plugged this in, it will over-ride all their security and you can access their info. Use the codes I sent in the text message and then delete the message. We may be immortal, but we're not indestructible. Enough humans find out what happened and come after us, we could be in trouble, so we can't be sloppy. Afterwards, if we do it right, they won't know their information has been lifted and we can put this database together."

"We're so high tech!" I laughed.

Darren grinned. "Of course! We're twenty-first century vampires using human technology to help ourselves."

Nathaniel clapped me on the back. "Don't worry, Anthony, we can always stalk our prey when we feel like reminiscing. But for the most part this isn't just about making our life easier—safer even. It's also about the global market. It's about survival, evolving. We can sell this technology and transform our species from primitive to modern. You're new to this world, but me, I've been hunting for centuries. I'll still do it occasionally; I enjoy it. But if I want I can just use this and then do something else with my time rather than stalk criminals. I've never told you, but I hate the cold, the rain, and this keeps me out of it," Nathaniel added.

Darren laughed. "Grandpa here needs it a bit easier!" Then his laughter stopped and his face was serious. "But guys, Julian and I will need these back straight after. Don't try and hack these. We got equipment that won't detect us. And the other important issue—I don't think we can just go in and kill a house full of people. Not without alerting people we don't want alerted. I think we'll just have to drain them almost and then re-condition their minds." He turned swiftly and jumped onto a small roof balcony and lifted the locked window easily.

"Is he busting locks?" I asked.

"Oh, don't worry. The mortals will fix them afterwards! Then we'll use the front door. Nobody will see us leaving."

We descended en mass into the building. Nathaniel and I decided to hunt out the delinquents together. I can't speak for what the others found within the flats of that huge place, but for us we found a pitiful state of human who would make any sane being—mortal or otherwise—want to drain his body of blood.

His soul full of anger, of fear that the result of which the room was filled with a gigantic wraith that screeched as we entered, but didn't react to us per say as we knew not to acknowledge it. Difficult as that was, I was now getting used to closing my mind off from others since being around my nephilim friends. A skill that was more precious than I realised at the time.

We kept righteous thoughts and feelings within us which was tricky as this pathetic excuse of a human and its crimes made me want to explode in a fury upon him and drain him slowly to death.

I've been told my entire life that I have an expressive nature and I am affected a lot by others actions. Now I was learning to control my emotions. And as in the beginning of my vampiric life, I had Nathaniel to aid me.

As we entered the damp tiny flat, the fiend stopped in his actions and looked at us with shock and abject horror. A plain looking man, plump from years of sedentary lifestyle, his face was non-descript, ugly as was everything about him. A loser. A nobody who only felt power in inflicting pain and suffering of others. No self-esteem, no pride. No soul. A waste of good air.

Most don't fight back, knowing on a subconscious level that we are the predators, they the prey and our strength is far greater, but also that they deserve this end. Often, our power radiates from us so much that they just freeze in fear. This man was no different.

Nathaniel took the criminal's left wrist, I took the right, and as the wretch crumpled under our joint bleeding of him, his wraith started to vanish, but not without screaming it's lament of its futile existence.

I left Nathaniel to recondition the human, to instil within him a new philosophy similar to a programme in a computer so that he'd never be capable of hurting or inflicting any pain on another, even in self-defence. He would become scared of his shadow.

For most this is easy, for the evil have no awareness of self, no intelligence. They are automatons, re-enacting their petty, nasty behaviours in a self-righteous manner. And they go from cradle to the grave without ever realising this.

You may wonder why we don't instil something more positive, but the truth is, we can't over-ride a criminals subconscious that well. It's easier to break them down, knowing they'll never harm another. Maybe a nephilim could do a true reprogramming, but there are so many like this fiend that it would be unreasonable to expect the nephilim to go about reprogramming all of them.

I hacked all his tech quickly, using the various USB's and the text that Nathaniel had sent me just before entering. Shoving them in my pocket, I turned around and found Nathaniel finished, the man on the floor dead instead of reprogrammed.

Nathaniel smirked. "Yeah, well, it's only one body and what we found here, I didn't want it to live."

I just nodded. I did the same these days with those that were really vile. "Let's dump it now before it stinks," I offered.

And so off we headed, up the hill beyond the city and into the surrounding countryside to bury the dead.

I felt there could be a chance that we could make progress without the need for the nephilim to call upon the higher beings. If we vampires could organise ourselves using Darren's app, could we wipe out most of the phantom apparitions and a lot of delinquents? I never worry about running out of blood. The human species is too rife with malevolence, and if only they knew their own true power, they could become so much more. But they don't. If Acacius didn't need to call the higher ones, we would have a better chance of survival.

But what of the non-evil mortals, whose hearts had merely turned sour due to the unhappiness of their lives? Drinking their blood to save their souls? Even *if* we did that, would that rid them of their wraiths, of their hatred, their fear?

Even if I could justify the morality of this, there were just so many.

I reflected on these thoughts with Nathaniel. He tilted his head to the side, frowning and wide-eyed. "Anthony, you really don't understand the threat of this situation. I applaud your compassion for the human soul, I *really* do. But their wraiths, this is *their* responsibility. There is a choice, there is *always* a choice. When I lived as a mortal, hundreds of years ago, I was lucky to have some fortune. But life then was meagre, filthy, disease ridden. People had no choices then. Today, here at least, they have a kingdom and if they choose self-imprisonment within their minds, then who am I to be their saviour. I don't want to see man destroyed by hate, by fear, I really don't. But you and I, even with our friends, cannot solve this problem on our own. For every human we see in doom, maybe five, ten more are as them elsewhere in this city. And with the veil thinning, these creatures are spilling through. How could we send them back?"

I nodded. There had to be an easier way. If the higher angels came, we all faced annihilation.

"We need to know *where* they are coming from. They live in the hearts of man, the soul. Acacius had said the veil was thinning and so they must be able to be sent back, if we cannot kill them all."

The Children

Anthony

HUNTING WITH NATHANIEL, Darren, and Marcus, we decided to take to the streets this busy Saturday night instead of using the Vamp app. Apparitions hung thick in the air like low hanging clouds. The apparition fog affected people, causing them to lose their senses, seeking refuge in alcohol, hoping that its promise of drunken ecstasy would be their salvation from the confusion and depression which had fallen upon them. As the people gorged themselves on the alcohol, confusing their senses more, the ghostly demons feasted upon the negative emotions that both they and the humans' methods of escape wrought.

With so much evil, more were attracted and I feared that there was too much to feast upon, gluttonous proportions, and there would be too many evil souls to contain. More vampires from neighbouring cities and towns had come to dine and tension grew between the supernatural species, unseen by the mortals.

Fights broke out over humans, petty and vicious. With the humans so drunk, they barely noticed. For us, my species drinking from mortals who are high and drunk affects us greatly in a similar way as it does humans. We feel heady and it can be to our detriment, but it can also be fun—to a point.

We found ourselves in a club where the pounding music reverberated through our bodies, and we sprawled out in the corner and watched a band hammering on their instruments as people jumped and threw themselves around in a frenzy of the music, fuelled by drink.

I was glad I had already eaten. Their scent, their blood thick in the air, and my senses high on that could make me rash and dangerous, as I had been in the beginning of this crazy vampire life. It was needed though, time away from the reality of the situation with only the spectres keeping our attention. We had almost learnt to ignore them.

After some hours of living vicariously through the drunk humans, we decided to head home. The streets were less busy now and we grew more relaxed than we had been in months.

Walking back to my flat, I came across a female vampire creeping around the entrance of a pub that was closing. There was something about her, something smelled different. She didn't look particularly different and she was dressed very casually in jeans, boots, coat, and short blonde hair. But there was definitely something odd about her.

I stood back and watched behind a building. That smell, I knew it, I'd smelt it before. She took her victim easily enough, but she led her off, fingers gripping mercilessly into the woman's neck. What was this new thing? I can understand taking her victim off the street. To drink her there would be suicide, but her behaviour, her constant checking, scanning around to see who or what was watching her, or what could threaten her was peculiar indeed. Most vampires, while cautious, were confident in their own abilities and didn't tend to look over their shoulders. I kept at a distance as I followed and my heart beat fast as my instinct told me there was something weird here.

Sure enough, after a short distance she took the woman into a building. At least I assumed it was her home, unless she's chosen a random building that was empty to use for safety. It's an unwritten rule.

I waited outside, waiting to pick up where she was in the building when I heard a sound that chilled my soul: A child crying. I shot up the building using ledges and indentations in the bricks to climb, my intuition guiding me to the room where this fiend was keeping a child. I waited outside the window, not daring to look in until I had calmed my breathing.

As I peered through I saw something I never knew existed. There, a child feasted on the drunken woman. But this was something else. Black feathered wings tinged crimson, luminous porcelain skin with fangs so large they were almost comical. Her hands! They didn't resemble hands at all, more claw like and this child gorged on her victim with a ferocity which was cruel and dangerous. From the side of the room the vampire and her nephilim lover watched over the child, pride beaming from their faces.

I jumped down, startled, my heart racing with fear and wonder. Now I was the one looking around, making sure that no one had seen me.

Fascinated and horrified at what I'd just witnessed, I felt I should tell the others. But then they'd kill the child, but then maybe they should? Vampire and nephilim, how could that be?

Yet this was just the newest development in my supernatural knowledge, which seemed to grow constantly.

A new species had emerged and it looked to be more powerful, more brutal than its parents.

I went to find Marcus and we wandered to the park to talk. I wouldn't speak of what I had seen yet, and I would keep my mind fixed on mundane matters.

Even in the parks, wraiths hovered over the criminals and in my heart, I longed for a fast solution.

We noticed fewer nephilim and vampires who were previously and blatantly paired up in the city now and I was suspicious about that. Something told me that a change was at hand.

Marcus was there, sitting casually on a park bench not looking too good. As I walked towards him, out of nowhere a woman stepped out of the shadows from the tree line in the park. We were taken aback, firstly because she took us by surprise and secondly because I had an uncanny feeling I knew her from another time.

"My name is Lauren. I have come with my friends, my kin to help you rid this place of the phantoms, the demons, and some of my kin..." She looked to Marcus. "Some of my kin are hoping, trusting that in return you can help us?"

"Your *kind* are mindless vicious killers, so why should I help you?" Marcus replied indifferently.

"We come in peace. Like you, we are locked into the trap of feeding on humans to survive and though most, like you, would rather die than kill the innocent, that hunger is as strong as yours, if not stronger. The pack I represent doesn't kill humans, and is trying to persuade others not to kill. You can't tarnish a whole species on the actions of a few."

"Hardly a few. Then your pack is a most unique one. You are all here?" Marcus nodded, completely calm.

"No, that would be foolish," she said quietly. She was about my age when I was turned, her dark blond hair touching her shoulders. Her hazel eyes twinkled, I could smell instantly that she was human, but she had a stronger scent on her, a musky woody scent.

Then I sensed *them* and an overwhelming urge to run seized me. I wondered why I had not smelt them before.

Marcus interjected, "Don't fear, Anthony. They come in peace. They are lycans. So, Lauren, how do you propose to help?"

"A few of our kind have studied and practised magic and are now able Necromancers. With your help, we are confident we can aid in sending these demons back to where they came from and seal the veil," Lauren offered.

"And how can we help you?" Marcus enquired casually.

"Many have had enough, but don't want to be damned into the void like these phantoms. We cannot easily die and our history—or so we've been told—of those who have tried, end up living in a worse state. Could you or your kin help them back to their mortal selves?"

Marcus's voice was compassionate and warm. "I am truly sorry that you have been mutated against your will. You must know that normally my kin would kill you on sight, and they are fully aware that you are killers beyond your choosing. We couldn't change you back, but even if we could, can you imagine how you would cope, psychologically, after all you have done, after all those deaths on your hands? A vampire would struggle mentally if changed back." Looking at me he added, "It cannot be done. Your salvation. That is an interesting question and one I have never been asked, or never contemplated. But what I will do is ask those who know more. If we can't help you, will you still help here?"

"Yes. We would ask a truce and are willing to help seal the veil. Maybe he could help? He had Emidius' blood. Maybe that could help us."

"It has made me stronger but I cannot help you find your salvation. Aside from our help, I wonder why you concern yourselves with these human affairs."

"That's simple. We've seen the increase in demons and the state of the humans is unhealthy for us, and remember, we were human before this. We still have fond memories."

I could feel their presence increase now. Although they weren't all here, there were many of them. They were hidden in the trees, protecting Lauren. I had to ask, "You're human? Why are you with them? I've seen you before, haven't I? When I collected my lover as she stood over the burning remains of her Maker, in the waste grounds outside Bath on the South of the city. That was over a year ago. You and these lycans were watching us in the tree line?"

"Which question to answer first?" She smiled. "I was led to aid them, but I am not their leader. It was a calling. It's easier having a mortal to negotiate. Yes, we saw you. We've been watching you for some time. You interest us; you're quite different from most vampires. And we hoped that your blood will help us."

"Them, you mean. Not you, not we. But lycans don't drink blood. Had you not considered seeking out the demi-god yourselves? And, I may add, I am surprised they'd risk your mortal life to contact us."

Lauren was undeterred by my comment that we could've harmed her and continued, "Emidius... If we could find her we would've asked her first, but we've never managed that. We'd risk being killed, but that's not something that would deter us."

A man stepped forward. He was well-built, tall, with shoulder-length dark hair, and a beard. He looked rugged and I knew at once this was their Alpha. Somehow, he was exactly as I imagined an Alpha would be. The stereotypical TV Alpha.

Marcus had a look of surprise, as did I that they would risk the life of a mortal over their own.

"No, you're both wrong. We wouldn't, I wouldn't. Had you made the slightest move to hurt her, I would've torn you apart."

At which point Marcus smirked at the audacity that a mere lycan could do such a thing. His voice was deep and he had a warmth about him, a protective, almost caring aura towards the human woman. He stood close to her, arms touching. Lovers, human and lycan.

This bold creature walked closer to Marcus, meeting his gaze, but kept a respectful distance. He watched Marcus but spoke to both of us.

"As Lauren said, we've been watching you—all of you. You are different from your kind; you have a conscience of a sort. Allow me to introduce myself, I am Sabian, and yes, I am the Alpha. The reason Lauren welcomed you was to put you at ease. If I had wandered out straight away you would have become immediately defensive. We didn't want that.

"I don't ask for help for myself. I've managed in the main to not kill my prey. And Anthony, we do not *eat* humans, we do indeed feed on their blood, just as you do. A fact that even Lauren wasn't aware of. It's just our wild and brutal temperament with the transformation means most," and here he lowered his voice, "most of our victims are mutilated. It has taken me many, many years to control this temperament and most cannot. Their primal hunger drives them to insanity and they never learn to master it. Some don't even care, but there are none like that with me. I have a high respect for humans. I am tortured that I have to feast on them for life. But you *know* that feeling, those conflicted emotions, that self-loathing, Anthony, do you not? That's in part what sets you apart from other vampires who never even question this. Except at first, when you were first made, but that's to be expected if not ideal."

"So you want me, my kin to help your...*pack*?" I always struggled to accept new paranormal species. I found this vaguely funny as I was also a figure of myth.

He nodded. "We'll meet again soon." And with that they left, fast, hand in hand.

With the help of the lycans, we would regain balance in our town. My biggest concern was what would happen to Marcus, and those of his kind who had crossed over to the darkness. My head told me Marcus wasn't my responsibility, yet, I couldn't help but hope for the best for him and his fallen brethren. We started to wander back to Acacius' home to see the other nephilim when Nathanial and Darren crossed our path, both grinning like children with an edge of excitement that was infectious.

"We were inspired after hearing that some vampires had been infected by *wraiths*," Darren explained, his voice high-pitched in exhilaration. "It seems they- the vampires- became so captivated by the wraiths when feasting on their human victims, that the wraiths consumed their dark vampire souls and became more physical! Well, it seems your angelic friend might well be right, if wraiths can consume the soul of a vampire, then do we not take the soul from our victims when drinking their blood?"

There it was again, the thing I didn't want to be true. But did vampires even have souls? He continued, "I'd always thought of nephilim as righteous creatures, bestowing their judgement most harshly on *vampires,* but it seems there is some truth in their beliefs."

Darren paused here to allow Marcus time to realise that he was in fact complimenting his kin, and then Nathaniel continued blurting out so fast I had a job following what he was saying. "Anyway, Darren and I were updating the app and we felt such enthusiasm to be ridding the world of the criminally insane. I don't know. Anyhow, we'd been working on it for some time. You were away at this time, yes I heard about it. You entered a portal? I've never done that so I want to know about it…Anyhow, my point, *we started to see them*. At first we thought it was the effects of some polluted blood perhaps, after all you never know what these mortals put into their bodies."

Darren interjected, "Tiny lights, orbs flashing, zooming around. Almost transparent, bright white or blue. We were stunned, I mean we vampires, the supposed *evil,* being visited by the elementals. I'd always accepted my dark fate, I had like many stuck to the rules to only drink from the wicked, the dispossessed, but I never thought of myself as *good*. Until now, now I feel like I can do something, be a part of something bigger than myself."

"Did they speak to you?" Marcus added.

"No," Nathaniel replied. "Though a few appeared to be almost tormenting us with their appearance. It's fascinating; in all my years I had never experienced this, nor expected it. Anyway, as we walked through the city with our new found findings, feeling powerful and righteous, we saw those wraiths of man's souls. We walked right up to the humans and whilst one of us engaged in conversation with the chosen human, the other stared right into the wraith and, it's hard to describe because it was instinctual, channelled powerful sublime energy into the thing."

Darren interrupted, "It disappeared! I mean it just went. And the man we picked started to come back to himself, so Nathaniel then channelled this energy into him also whilst I distracted him with meaningless conversation. We tried a few more, and though some were harder to get rid of, it worked. Can you imagine the possibilities this has? And then we found you here."

"This is interesting indeed." Marcus laughed. "So, you suppose that you will do me out of a job, huh? Your species evolves and finds greater meaning than just the lust for blood. Whatever happens and however few of your kind learn this, it warms my soul that out of my mistake which has led to this awful state, I know others who are finding solutions. I'm happy for you. You will no doubt use this on your victims, maybe instilling them with good? It must be tried, I think?"

It sounded unlikely to me, but I didn't want to spoil their revelation. I had the feeling there was something else at work here, something they weren't aware of. Maybe the elementals were still with them and using their power to rid the human of

the thing. It was exciting though, but the task was still moun-
tainous as there were so many wraiths and demons. If the others could do this, that would be great and maybe more would
join them. I knew from meeting with Darren and his friends
that most vampires were alarmed at the situation. So much
darkness breaking through the veil and some had even been enwrapped by these entities whilst feeding on their human victims. How that happened, my only idea was they became entranced by the wraiths, as I had done when I first encountered
them. Luckily for me, Acacius had told me how to avoid becoming engaged with them, knowledge I'd relayed in passing.
This knowledge needed to be spread amongst the community.

"We will meet with you gentlemen later. Now the elementals are here, that will help. They cannot be harmed in the
process as they're not physical like us, they are pure energy."
Marcus spoke softly, his voice echoing around the empty park
and we made our way back to Acacius.

"Actually, I'm going home and I'll meet with you and
Acacius later," I said in a weary voice. "So we have Darren
and Nathaniel, maybe others, the fire crystal—whatever that'll
do—and the wolves."

"You don't look happy, considering we are growing a formidable force."

"In my heart I don't think it's enough. And you, I'm worried for you. You keep...changing. That's my fault. If I hadn't
gone to find her."

"What's done is done. I was never designed to take such
tainted blood. I think drinking you with Emidius's has sus-
tained me longer. But enough of that for now, others may help,

I feel it. I am sure they are coming. You also need to contact your old friends, Nicolas who you rescued? He may be helpful."

I doubted that. I was protective over Nicolas simply because he was so meek, but maybe Marcus was right. Maybe he could help. And I would look at what others could do to help. We needed it. Walking back, the people looked like something from macabre art, grey, hunched, almost lifeless.

The phantoms were thick like smoke blocking out the moonlight, in the sunlight. News reporters made up fake news about the cause, and scientists scrambled for any theory that the establishment would believe. I wondered if the human authorities really knew, some of them at least, what was happening. But maybe they liked it, obedient humans, too sick to argue but alive enough to control. It was almost like a zombie film, and I hate zombies.

Secrets

Marcus

AFTER ANTHONY LEFT, I stole back into the park, calling out for Lauren and Sabian.

I hadn't had the chance to meet up with Sabian since my encounter with Luke, the dragon shifter but I didn't want to share this information with my vampire friend, knowing that shifters tend to be a secretive breed and it wasn't my information to spill out anyway.

"I came across Luke, some weeks back," I confessed as they walked towards me, Sabian's face was full of intrigue, his eyes narrowed with interest. He nodded slightly.

"I saw him transform," adding quickly, "I haven't told a soul. I followed him leaving a club, he'd been staring at me, but there was something about him, something different then watching him run- his gait was unusual. Will he fight with us?"

Sabian took a deep breath and looked at Lauren whose expression revealed nothing.

"Tell me, what did you see?" he asked.

I knew why he asked me this, he wanted to know if I was calling his bluff, we immortals are an untrusting lot. "He's a dragon shifter. He would be a huge help in our fight, so will he join?"

"He wants to, but..." he paused. "I know he would be a great asset, but his kind, a dragon shifter is rare. I have advised him not to. Too many would become aware of his...abilities and he could be persecuted because of that. Your kin," again Sabian shook his head, his face frowning with worry, "The nephilim who are untainted would make it their mission to hunt him down. And if they, or any other immortal kill him whilst he is transformed into the beast, they would use the blood of that beast- and no doubt the head for all kinds of weird magic. And to boast. Most don't believe in dragons, for good reason. For Luke, and any other like him, I fear his existence depends upon discretion. That's why I welcomed him into our pack, and every member swore a blood oath to keep his identity a secret. An oath which I now must insist you take."

"I am happy to take the oath Sabian. I swear, too, that I haven't told anyone." I looked out towards the park, the normality of the place looked peaceful, but what it held- ancient secrets, strange creatures. I wondered what it must be like to be born human and to never know of this other world that coexisted in secret.

Sabian drew out a dagger from under his coat and handed it to me.

Bone handle, my hand tingled as I held it, a talisman of power. Light-headedness suddenly sent me stepping back, that strange sensation of merging into nothing and everything, but I tightened my grip around the dagger and cut clean across my right palm.

His eyes narrowed as he watched, looking from me to Lauren and I quickly handed him the knife.

"What has happened to you? Is this the result of drinking vampire blood?" His voice raised in alarm.

"Maybe. But there are other things, take the knife- my blood should not harm you." His expression did not look convinced, so I continued as the blood spilled from my palm.

"I followed Anthony into a portal, he was looking for his lover." Breathing deeply and tensing my legs to steady myself, "I am the first nephilim to enter a portal. Or drink vampire blood. Everything is catching up. Don't be alarmed, look I am willing to take your blood oath. But my strength is leaving me- I feel it."

"His blood may harm yours Sabian? Nephilim blood scorches the insides of vampires!" Lauren added alarmed.

"It may do," he spoke calmly. "But honour and trust are worth dying for, what kind of a leader am I to refuse to do what I asked him to do?"

Slicing his palm, blood trickling, we locked hands letting the blood lines fuse together. A rush of wild energy surged through me, primal and strong. Watching him, his eyes widened, mouth open as my tainted blood mixed into his.

"I hope my blood brings you some power, Marcus. You're unlike any nephilim I've ever come across. Know that you are always welcome in my pack. I'm all too aware that most lycans are vicious and brutal, mine are not."

As I spoke, "Thank You," he acknowledged my thanks with a smile and left swiftly holding hands with his human, Lauren.

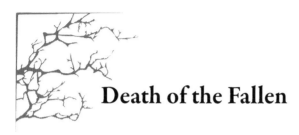

Death of the Fallen

Anthony

MARCUS LOOKED AWFUL. I was at his rented apartment. He was curled up in a ball on his bed and so fragile. His form was solid, then for a flash transparent. Gone was that beautiful face, high cheek bones, wide grin and full lips with shining dark eyes. He was crumpled and contorted in pain.

I bent over him and stroked his forehead. Bloody sweat covered him and he seemed barley aware of my presence. Groaning and crying, he was in a fever so deep that I knew in my heart his life was fading.

The others looked on. Acacius ever the nurturer hadn't left his side, after I had left Marcus in the park his health had taken a sudden downturn within hours. Fortunately, they had rushed to his side, and within a day here I was watching my friend dying.

Acacius placed a damp cloth to his friend's face. No one wanted to speak, no one wanted to face the reality of living without this radical, charismatic and passionate being. *Couldn't the fire crystal help? After all it was to get rid of evil.*

Acacius, hearing my thoughts, smiled at me and touched my arm in compassion. Quietly he spoke, "No, Anthony. It would indeed take away the impurity. However, it is so deeply ingrained within him that it would take him as well. And much as I love my brother, that is for a bigger cause. There is nothing we can do here except be with him. The only reason he managed to survive so long was, I think, thanks to you."

"Marcus, always reckless, always the rebel. Why did he have to be such a fool?" Halina mumbled shaking her head. She sounded angry and she was. She was angry at having to lose her friend and angry at him for doing this and for leaving them. I understood. She stood rigid, arms folded, trying to contain no expression on her face, but there were tears in her eyes. They had all known each other for perhaps centuries and that bond is hard to lose, especially in a world of the short-lived mortals whose lifetime was just a flicker to the nephilim.

One day I might experience this with others, but I had already felt a strong bond forming between my immortal friends, especially Marcus, my first nephilim friend. Immortality makes you feel like you're living on an alien planet with the short-lived. A great chasm builds as you can no longer relate to them, their petty squabbles and anger when they don't realize just how fleeting their lives are. In a heartbeat their lives will be at the end. Although I had only been immortal a short while, I understood this, I felt it in my core.

But then my mind was rambling, anything to divert it from the reality facing me. *Marcus, I had tasted your Divine blood and I have loved you as a brother.*

Tears ran down my face and I needed to be near that once larger than life man. I felt ashamed then, that when I first met him I was intimidated by him and suspicious of his intent towards Rachel. I think I found it all too much, losing Rachel and now Marcus. Soon Acacius and his friends would be gone if we could rid the humans of their demented ghouls. Nathaniel was with his friends he'd known for half a century. I would be alone for the first time in my life. Alone without friend's, immortal and empty.

At that moment all my hope, my strength left me. I clung to the fire crystal as I watched him, my fingers tight around it, it didn't just represent an end to the Hell breaking through, but something deeper to me. Something personal. My memory of the adventure we had shared in that frozen place, that portal that only he and I experienced. And knowing I would have to give it up, knowing that all I would have left were fading memories, my eyes welled, my mouth became parched and the emptiness in my stomach grew.

The others fell silent as he stopped moving, ceased all sound. The room darkened and a chill swept through, the cold of death. Involuntarily I gasped as a flash of blue white light burned harsh and fast, then the darkness lifted and he was gone. And I knew in my heart he had indeed been damned.

The flash of fire, the darkness, and then complete emptiness. No one could speak. Aaron stood looking out of the window with Halina, his arm wrapped around her.

They were bracing themselves against their emotions and Acacius and I couldn't look at each other, it was too much, but we slumped down beside the bed together and all sat in silence for hours. I was glad I had known him, and them. In time, serenity settled in place of the doom, and the rain turned to sunlight, hot through the window. Our minds fell into philosophical daydreams, as happens at the death of a loved one.

Without a word, Acacius got up quietly and offered me a hand. I took it and we walked silently out into the new day, a new beginning to see what would come at us next.

After a week, we started to find other nephilim suffering the same fate as Marcus, only things became worse. The mortals were distinctly more zombie-like, and some seemed barely conscious enough to keep themselves alive. It was as if they were just living out their existence, going through the motions, so to speak with little awareness, lifeless. Their pallor was grey, eyes bleak, and the streets were virtually empty. A lot of the shops were closed, and as I read the papers, the authorities insisted that it was due to a mystery virus to hide the truth. As far as I could tell, it was at least localised at present and hadn't spread too far outside the city.

I guessed some at the top knew what was really happening, but were clueless on how to stop this.

It was creepy walking through the tiny city. Not that long ago I thought we were the creepy ones, but now the mortals looked like the phantoms that leeched from them, draining their life force.

I hoped that with the help of others we could stop this, send them back and close the veil, but there were not many of us and loads of mortals. Like fighting a zombie army that you don't want to kill, and with only a dozen of you.

Melancholy fell heavy on us. It was hard to concentrate, hard to care, and an emptiness made me feel hollow inside. I was on autopilot. I know the others felt this, too, by their actions, by how we were talking to each other. Without emotion, stiff, holding in our feelings.

As I walked through the city in this dejected manner, the wraiths were immediately attracted to me, and to be honest I didn't give a fuck about them and their petty evils. Had they been solid I would have drained every last one of them in anger.

We needed a ploy though, a way to gather as many drained mortals as possible to one place and I still had little idea how the fire crystal would work. I hoped Acacius and Halina had figured that out, otherwise I'd just be a twat holding an unusual crystal amongst chaos and evil!

When I arrived at Acacius's home it was full of other nephilim, but not nephilim like him, Aaron, and Halina, but pure nephilim. As Acacius led me in, introducing me to the others, it was clear that most of them were not pleased to see me.

They were stalwart and striking, their fair skin vivid against the black leather clothing. All of them wore this. At first glance their attire looked regular, if somewhat rebellious, but close up much of it was padded with long strips of reinforced leather, and built in chain mail ending in strong boots. Modern-day armour.

Tall, like the others, their confidence was tangible and they looked at me with indifference. I saw many different weapons such as swords and axes. Some held what looked like silver wands but these wands gave off a faint white glow. Male and female, all had striking features, luminous skin, slate-grey eyes, and lithe but strong physiques. I felt like a hobbit in a room full of Elves, *that* was not a feeling of empowerment.

We crammed into the living room, which was small anyway. There must have been about thirty of them. Everyone was silent and looking at Acacius, Halina, and Aaron, faces stern. They were ready for action.

Acacius paused. They knew why they were here and now it was time to plan. He opened a small wooden box and presented the fire crystal. Upon doing this there was a gasp amongst them.

He nodded his head towards me. "Anthony found this, or rather it found him. You know it requires the Divine light to activate it, and we need that now. We have been researching a way to draw the mortals, demons, and wraiths into a single place to destroy them. In fact, we want to destroy the evil that is draining the infected mortals completely. Just sending it back through the veil is not our intention now. Evil will still persist, as long as mortals hold hate and fear in their hearts, but here in this tiny city we can at least hope to cleanse those who emit it."

"That is a noble cause indeed, Acacius." One of his kin stepped forward. He was lithe with dark hair, strapped in armour, and his face told a thousand tales. Possibly older than the others, his stance was solid and his presence potent. "But there are only a few dozen of us, and the demons continue to crawl their way through. And the fallen of our kind..." He shook his head. "They need to be held accountable for their despicable actions. With them still alive and drinking blood, this will only continue to hold open the door to evil. It sickens me that Marcus has brought this upon all, with his selfish and thoughtless action, but I see no other way. Whilst they live, I think we cannot win." His eyes were full of sorrow as he spoke. The others whispered amongst themselves before Acacius spoke again.

"There may be no need of that, for as we speak, Marcus has died. It seems that by tasting the dark blood they have sealed their own fate. I know others are suffering the same fate. We will sweep the city, and confirm this."

The other nephilim spoke again. "With them gone, we have a better chance of ridding the place of these iniquitous beings. Have you called for higher assistance?"

"Yes. We all have. And we have found an incantation to draw the evil to a single place. That includes the mortals' infected by their own hatred. We have to aim not to kill the mortals, but it will be, what it will be. Their fate is by their own design."

"What of the vampires who paired with our kin? We cannot allow them to live, surely. That would be abhorrent."

"We kill them first. With our infected kin dying or dead, it should be easy enough. They at least cannot survive our blood."

The dark-haired nephilim stepped forward, facing me and looking to Acacius. "But he has tasted Marcus's blood and probably others. I should kill him where he stands!"

I was taken aback and fear rose quickly. Surrounded by these immortal creatures, I would never stand a chance. To add to my horror, Acacius added, "You are right, you should, but Anthony has his own destiny to meet and Emidius *chose* to save him. Without her blood, he wouldn't have survived drinking our blood." He paused and I panicked, then he continued. "He was led to the fire crystal and he alone will need to carry it. Remember, Leland, there has to be a balance here. As you see him as evil, so the Divine sees *us, you* as Fallen. It has always seen the nephilim as fallen from Heaven, by the very fact that we are here, in man's domain unable to leave.

"And I, *we* encouraged Anthony to drink from Marcus. He is now no ordinary vampire, he possess the strength and knowledge of both Emidius and Marcus. We hoped that making him extraordinary he could help seal the veil between demons, wraiths, and man. We knew we could not win this fight alone. *How* Anthony uses this power will determine his fate. And I have other news that concerns me."

Leland was clearly not convinced and eyed me with anger, I knew at some point he would disregard Acacius's words and kill me in an instant if I was caught off guard.

"What of the other news that concerns you? What do you speak of?" Leland replied angrily.

Acacius, divine as he was, lied. "It is only a suspicion, a thought, and until I am sure I will say no more."

But I knew he meant the children.

And so, that night a small group, myself included, went out to investigate the fate of the nephilim. The fire crystal would be used as a beacon to attract the evil and those trapped in its wake.

Gathering of the Damned

Anthony

THEY CROUCHED ON TOP of the Georgian buildings, their massive wings beating slowly. Looking down below as the mortals passed unawares these magnificent and terrifying creatures watching and waiting. Waiting for their fix, their once milky skin, now shining obsidian, crimson tinged from the blood that they stole, blood that they were not designed to take. Scarlet that glistened under the moon, like something from a Gothic tale, hands gripped on the stone and their movements' slight and animal like, though they'd never been human.

Jumping down one by one, they blended into the city effortlessly. Their wings were invisible to mortal eyes, some magic they held. I stayed hidden otherwise they'd kill me for sure. They'd smell me and bleed me dry.

Powerful giants with the confidence of a hundred kings, each of them were forbidden and not answerable to anyone, not now. They searched my kind, my kin who they'd spent thousands of years killing remorselessly. Others of their kin who had not fallen still had humanity, but these ones who had fallen into savagery had changed in a frenzy of the blood lust. That feeling, that swoon, hungry and brutal. And so my vampire kin, the hunter, become the hunted.

I thought my pounding heart would explode and I wished I had my friends with me. Death would fill the streets tonight. Blood would be spilled and all the damned were crawling through stealing the souls of men and destroying their hearts.

And I had thought I could awaken from my secret crypt three months after the war of the immortals to find peace. Evidently I could not. In the realm of the supernatural, nothing rests for long...

And then the demons came. Dozens of them, most beautiful to look at, and that, like the vampire was their weapon. But I saw the oblivion in their dead eyes and smelled the death that they carried always with them. I wanted to kill them all. After taking my lover, I would only rest once I had wiped out the demons and the wraiths. But my ego held more confidence than I. In short there were so many and cowardly as it was, my fear grew as I waited there.

They had a power untold. Something so malicious about them, so cruel it was monstrous. A chill ran over me as I spied them, as they lingered and followed people but the people didn't see them.

Fear rushed through, gripping tightly to my body, my limbs and stilting my breathing as I waited there on my own, the fire crystal tucked tightly in my coat pocket. Waiting for Aaron, Halina, and Acacius. Then, Nathaniel arrived and had mustered his vampire friends and they were using the app Darren created to find more to fight these demonic beings. They had managed to muster dozens of vampires to destroy the wraiths of men, though we were all still unsure how this would work. Acacius was bringing his purebred nephilim warriors and soon the centre of the city would be a battle ground against good and evil, or evil and worse evil to be correct. So I jumped into the battle, yelling loudly now that my friends had arrived.

Ghouls had been superseded by banshees and every supernatural creature I had ever read about in fairy tales as a child it seemed had gathered there as if invited to Armageddon. Maybe they sensed us and so gathered on mass. Maybe we'd die, but it didn't matter.

Humans were drained of their energy to such extent that we were their only hope. Their government ruled by the Elite, unbeknownst to them, had been fed lics about this. Though now the Elite were smaller and scattered, or so Nathaniel had told me.

It was ironic really. If humans knew we existed they'd wage a war on us overnight and hunt us like the medieval witch trials. But either way, we had to help them. For me it was compassion, but for others perhaps, without them, our kind would die. And I couldn't allow that.

And so I waited...

I couldn't believe it. In the distance walking towards this centre of death the shape of one so timid, so meek that courage and fear for him warmed my heart simultaneously. Nicolas! How the hell would he fight here? But his bravery was almost enough to make me weep. He was such a timid character!

But then I saw *her* and my breath stopped. Rachel was walking behind him with creatures that seemed almost transparent. Shadow creatures, lost souls...there were many of them. I wanted to run to her, but that would have been stupid, running into the thick of all this evil. She looked changed, her countenance, her eyes. A power emitted from her that was tangible and dark. I took a step back and gasped. I knew in that instant she had killed the demon Lucius and she was now forever changed. Hollow even. I was happy beyond words to see her but her countenance, her stern face, instinct telling me she had changed greatly. But there was no time to contemplate.

She and Nicolas grabbed at the demons and bled them, casting them aside like trash when done. They worked together, the demons attacking them fiercely, contorted faces of hate and yet Nicolas and Rachel mimicked them, mocking them before swiftly grabbing at them with such speed and biting, drinking, draining.

Their shadowy friends used the opportunity to snatch at demons and consume them into their very bodies, like a low cloud passing through a forest. The demons and wraiths both vanished, screaming as they became once more, nothingness.

Nathaniel and his friends on seeing Rachel and Nicolas bleed demons, also began to drink their blood. Acacius, Halina, and Aaron and their warriors arrived and fought like soldiers, slaying these vile demonic creatures with their swords. But still more seemed to pour in, as though the more that were killed, the more appeared.

I bit and bled as many as I could, and saw the humans in the outskirts of the battle completely unawares. Some were being dragged in by wraiths and used as bait, and I and others kept pushing the humans back out. But it was as if some were attracted to it on a subconscious level. Attracted and drawn to death.

As we seemed to be losing, our hope and energy started to drop, but we couldn't let it.

Fighting in the square beside the Abbey, it was like being in a portal, the world outside carried on as normal but here, Hell was loose and rampant. At first I didn't see them, but as I looked to Nathaniel and his vampire friends, I started to see miniscule flashes of light hovering around them, piercing the wraiths that had been drawn here by the spell of the fire crystal. The tiny elementals, their faces spiteful, were laughing as they consumed the wraiths, the hate of man, and disappeared just as fast.

A massive lycan, half-wolf half-man, jumped beside me and tore off the head of a demon and I breathed a huge sigh of relief and shock. I knew in my gut that it was Sabian, the pack leader, always the largest of the lycans. They had come. Snarling and drooling with blood on their fur, these beasts were frighteningly powerful.

Acting on animal instinct, they cut through these damned creatures and now we seemed to be making progress. I couldn't stop though my body was weary and I could hear my heart beating loud and fast. Sharp, short breaths and I was out of energy. Then I spied it.

In amongst the crowded mass of phantoms and demons, a formidable, winged demon saw me and made straight for me. His voice was deeper, thundering as he approached. Skin dark and glistening crimson with the sweat of blood this giant with a face half-human, half monster, and a body and legs many times larger than a nephilim. He wore platinum arm bands and some scant clothing, as if it never occurred to him to cover up. His sheer mass was threatening, and as if his size wasn't enough his wings were massive, crimson black leather looking, and my breathing turned to panting, sharp, and shallow as fear petrified me to the spot.

He spoke directly and very slowly to me, "Come to me!"

His pace was strong and so fast. His long legs rushed forward, not human but some half-animal/ half human thing that just to look at filled me with dread. He picked me up, and in my terror my body and my strength was as useless as a rag doll, limp and powerless. My heart stopped as shock and terror washed over me.

"You *are* the bringer of Death. Do not assume you are something better. Your light is brightest. I have waited for you. I am the Angel of your death."

His voice was guttural and penetrating. I felt his rancid breath on my face as he held me to him, his face inches away. "If you refuse me, refuse your fate, your death, your future is eternity in isolated darkness."

His awful wings beating fast, creating a current of their own, he lifted me into the sky and continued, "You with *her* blood. You with the crystal of fire, drinker of souls, chosen. Come to destroy *me*!" His laugh was terrible and deafening, rolling his head back. Then looking at me with those devilish eyes of blood he announced, "Welcome home, my child of Lucifer!" He pierced my neck fiercely—such huge fangs—draining me so fast that my head spun like a whirlwind.

When I came around I was on the floor, in my haze I thought I saw another huge black shadow circling around then diving down like a bullet towards this devil who had dropped me. Like a serpent, massive wings pulled pack, a yell like the cry of all the vanquished souls in Hell, as it opened its mouth and poured forth fire.

I must have hit my head, rubbing my eyes, in the next instant, the devil who attacked me was shielding his eyes.

Firebolts of white light bursting out of the black sky like nuclear explosions, illuminating the Abbey square in flashes so that all here, angel or demon covered their eyes from the blast.

I struggled to open my eyes against this blazing white-gold light. The illumination was so gigantic that it covered the sky completely, like a divine roof for the Abbey and beyond. And the sound! Booming bass reverberating so that even the walls of the Abbey seemed to shake. I thought my ears were bleeding.

Another star-burst flared so intense that all again shielded their eyes. As it dimmed slightly, the centre was white, with gold tails scorching off, looking almost like feathers made of fire. A tiny dark centre appeared and the whole thing swooped low.

Acacius grabbed my arm, shouting for me to bring out the fire crystal over the noise of the pandemonium. I scrabbled in my pocket, worried that maybe it had broken in the chaos. My hands struggled to grip it. I was still shaking intensely after that thing had drained me, that thing which terrified me still. The crystal was intact and with Acacius holding my arm, I held it up.

This star was immediately drawn to it, to me and attached a beam of blistering light to it. Penetrating the crystal, the blue flame inside grew instantly and blazed out with the white-gold beam, bursting out heat, with the intensity of luminosity.

All had stopped in the presence of this blazing glow. Acacius looked reverently at it.

"Seraphim," he whispered to me.

Then the lights mixed with a flash and fell onto everything and the demons, wraiths, and ghouls vanished, consumed in the light. The Angel of Death who had grabbed me was on his knees but the Seraphim consumed him, too, slowly. He looked like he was melting, his skin liquefying and his huge wings on fire.

As I reluctantly took my eyes off this Divine light, all the nephilim were on their knees in respect. Nathaniel had joined them and looked on in awe.

As the huge creature dissolved roaring as the pain seared through its repugnant body, blackness fell. The air was pitch black and icy wind blew. Fear sent a shiver though me.

Within seconds, the light returned to normal, the street lights with their white cool glow and everything sounded and looked normal.

As I got up unsteadily, Acacius came over and offered me his arm. Shock and relief filled our expressions, and like soldiers after battle we hugged each other.

Nicolas wearily came over to me, followed by Rachel who looked strong, terrifying even, but serene.

Nathaniel and his friends looked around, staring in fascination at both the lycans and the shadow people.

The slain had vanished. Nothing remained except us. We all huddled together, vampire, nephilim, shadow people and lycan alike. No one spoke. No one wanted to break the silence.

And in the distance, from around the back of the Abbey we saw a small number of children approach us. But not human children, they only looked barely human.

My mind instantly recognized them. These were the off-spring of the nephilim and their vampire mothers. And with them was Rachel's strange friend, Damien. And alongside them, Lauren, Emidius, Jamie, and Marcus.

The End.

Book 3: Children of the Fallen Taster

Always Dark Angel Series.
Anthony.

THE VEIL BETWEEN THE living and the dead had been sealed and I was left standing in the aftermath of demons and the wraiths of man's hatred, now gone, and taken into the oblivion of Light by the Seraphim. Many had come together—vampires, nephilim, elementals and lycans—to fight the darkness that was destroying man, and with the divine help summoned by the nephilim we had succeeded.

Sighing heavily, I looked on at my once human lover, Rachel. She had fought in the battle and had changed beyond belief. Our eyes met, my heart trembled, and she gave me a small, friendly smile before darting her eyes away.

A small tremor of dejection beat through me, my legs trembled as a wave of heat swept over me from the battle that had just ended.

The purebred nephilim were gone, only our half bred nephilim friends remained, which gave me solace. At least I wouldn't be on my own without her. On my own and immortal. My worst fear.

As I turned my glance to the new situation which caused silent confusion amongst us, running my fingers through my matted hair and wiping the bloody sweat from my face, blinking rapidly at what I saw.

In the distance stood Marcus, my close nephilim friend. But we had all watched him die and mourned his loss heavily. He was with Emidius, a strange demi-god who took on human form when dealing with similar creatures, and next to her Jamie, my comrade from a war we had been caught up in two years past.

My mouth dropped open as my mind registered Marcus, but my heart told me to be cautious unless it was a trick. I forgot to breathe for a few minutes and my body was tense, but as his eyes caught mine, he beamed the biggest smile I'd ever seen. My exhaustion turned to excitement in that instant, adrenalin coursing through me.

"Marcus!" I called. I rushed towards him, bloody tears streaming down my dirty face. My face hurt, my smile was so wide. He looked different. Still dark, his wings like midnight and slate grey eyes but restored, vibrant, at ease. We hugged, and I held him fast with so much happiness.

But before I could say anything else Emidius bellowed, "Jamie and I have saved your renegade friend Marcus." Pausing now that she had our attention she added, "There is a price."

I thought, *there always is...*

Raising her voice louder, she said, "You will establish yourselves and create order from this chaos. I helped you before and *this* turmoil was the result of my assistance. Sort yourselves out, Marcus will help. You will establish a Council of the Supernatural. Each race will have two representatives. Failure to do this will be your own demise. Frankly, I am sick of clearing up your messes—that includes you nephilim. See to it."

As she turned to leave, her proud head held high, I caught Jamie's glance, and took the opportunity to see him. She carried on without him. God, I was glad he was stubborn and stayed behind. We had been through Hell together, and as I surveyed my friend, he held out his hand and we embraced.

"Where have you been? Can you tell me? I've missed you," I spluttered.

"Everywhere! I'm not the same as I was. I'm not flesh and bone although I may seem it. I know I feel solid, I don't quite understand it all myself. I've been to different parts of reality." Whispering, he added, "I'm not even sure I'm allowed to say."

"You're happy?" I asked.

"Very. And you? I see no change in her." He glanced at Rachel.

"No, but I have my friends. I'm not alone."

"You'd never need to be, remember that. I have to go, but we'll catch up soon."

"How do I contact you?"

"I knew you'd ask that. Here, take this."

He handed me what looked like an amulet, an oval shaped pewter disk with a strange creature and some ancient looking writing. The figure in the middle had a lion's head, human body, and snakes for legs and held up a wand in its right hand. I had no idea what the writing said or where it was from, and didn't have time to ask him.

"Take this, keep it safe. If you need me, focus on me, my face, myself whilst clasping it in your right hand. Do not let this get into the wrong hands, it's very old and irreplaceable. It was great to see you." Patting my shoulder, his face was animated as he headed off for another adventure. Jamie was always so lucky.

But that wasn't the end of our astonishment. Damien, Rachel's strange vampire friend, arrived with some children. Children born from vampire and nephilim—dark nephilim-that is those who had turned away from their celestial heritage and had taken to drinking blood from vampires, as Marcus had. Those nephilim and vampires were now dead, the purebred nephilim killed them as an abomination against nature. But the children had escaped? I didn't know how and though I feared those devilish infants, I was too overcome with joy to see my friend to question anything much.

One of the children had grown at a dramatic rate since I'd spied her along with others, and their appearance startled me. Black feathered wings that were much too big for them, large eyes with crimson pupils, and hands so claw like they bare-ly resembled that of their paranormal parents. They were dis-turbingly quiet and the vampire, Damien, obviously some hold over them.

My estranged lover, Rachel looked on at Damien, their eyes met and my heart crumbled in that moment. All was lost, he, whoever *he* was, had stolen her love from me. Anger and loss compounded me and I turned away.

Nathaniel, forward and brash as ever, shaking his head, stared in absolute horror at the children, blurting out, "Who in Hell are these? What *are* these?"

I turned away because I couldn't help but chuckle at his complete incompetence in the situation, it was comical. He al-ways knew how to put his foot in his mouth. Sad for the kids for sure, but he had now made an enemy of them no doubt! As I glanced to see who would answer, I noticed the children looked at him with loathing.

Damien remained calm, compassionate even. "These, my friend, are the Cambion, though not true Cambion. A new species, hybrids from vampire and nephilim with all the strengths of both and none, let me assure you, none of their weaknesses."

Everyone was silent, except Acacius who had kept his knowledge about them a secret, as I had.

Nicolas stepped forward, a huge smile spread across his face, "Well, well." He walked over to them having lost all his fear in the battle just fought, and placed his hand on the smaller of the two boys. The two boys were holding joining hands; the girl was holding Damien's other hand.

Nicolas was a natural and not condescending. Being turned vampire at an older age than most, his plump frame, receding hairline and plain features made him the picture of a *supernatural uncle*. Everyone needs an uncle like him. He was genuine. It amazed me that one could live so long a vampire, having seen so much death and having forcibly been a part of genocide, and yet he had maintained empathy.

Smiling, he spoke to them. "A new species? How fascinating! We will help as much as we can, but we cannot do anything unless you help us to understand you."

The children's faces grinned back at him and I saw their tightened postures relax a little.

Me, I wasn't so sure. Having spied one before, I knew their appetite for death and they would indeed need guidance. They were growing at an astonishing rate. The girl I'd seen a few weeks prior had grown already in human terms of many years. They would become formidable. And my intuition told me, if we didn't gain some control they could indeed be a threat to all species.

Damien spoke, "We will need a place to stay." As he said this he was looking at Nathaniel who had the largest place, a beautiful Georgian town house in the centre of the city. Nathaniel's brow furrowed, his jaw dropping open before adding quickly,

"I think the place that the nephilim reside in would be more suitable, I am not a child person. Acacius, you're from the divine, I think you and your nephilim friends would be aptly suited to help these children. But how in the hell are we to get them there without being seen?"

Acacius dismissed Nathaniel's words with a flick of the wrist, "Easy, don't worry about that." He strode towards Marcus, "What happened? We thought you were dead?"

"I don't know, everything went black and cold. The next time I was aware, Emidius and Jamie were standing over me. It is truly a gift to see you brother!" And they embraced, smiles filling their faces.

Aaron and Halina waited for their turn to hug Marcus. Few words could express our happiness at having our friend back. And I knew instinctively that Emidius would not reveal what magic she had conjured to bring him back. I, for one, didn't care. He was back and that was the main thing.

"Well, let's get these children home," Acacius bent a little to address these cambion. Then straightening up he asked, "Damien, I believe? I need to speak to you since you are the one looking after these young creatures," Acacius added.

Damien answered the questions before they were asked. "As with their parents, these children appear to mortals as human children. Humans only see what they want to believe."

Watching them discuss the future of these hybrids, I was fascinated in the power shift. Nicolas used to be a weak and frightened character but had now stepped up to helping these souls, and Nathaniel was clearly doing his best to shirk all responsibility. I smirked, I'd never seen him as a father figure.

Rachel was silent and weighing up the situation as I was, it being much bigger than it seemed. At their rate of growth, I guessed it would be less than a year until they reached adulthood. What then? Who knew? But whatever was between her and this Damien, I was glad he and Acacius had assumed responsibility and seemed to have control over them.

Me, I'm not the father type either...

These children could potentially wreak havoc, but I stopped my thoughts racing ahead. They, like their nephilim parents, could probably hear thoughts, and I didn't want to express my fears into something that they could manifest.

Sabian, the alpha leader of the lycans, had already run to his human lover, Lauren, and they watched in fascination as the future of this new species played out in front of them. I wondered who the man was in the group of lycans. He looked strikingly different from them, and yet had a semblance of lycan about him. I had noticed that he kept glancing at me, but he avoided eye contact and seemed anxious that I might catch his gaze.

I made my way over to him and asked gently, "Do I know you? I have the feeling we've met."

At first, he averted his gaze, then changed his mind. "My name is Jason, we haven't met, but I was held captive as you were in the Elite's war. I was one of the unfortunate ones changed into an experimental when the gene therapy went wrong." He paused to breathe, then his words spilled out, "I was taken in by Sabian and turned into a lycan- that's why I look different. I'd heard about you, I'd wanted to meet you. And Marcus."

I smiled. "It's a pleasure, Jason." I shook my head in disbelief at his sheer strength and determination to survive. "After all you've been through, it should be me wanting to meet you! That's an incredible feat." Turning away I called, "Marcus, come meet Jason!"

Rachel was avoiding eye contact. Weakness and pain gripped my stomach. I wanted to hold her, to kiss her, but she made it clear with her dismissive body language that my feelings wouldn't be reciprocated. But she *was* interested in Damien for sure, so to save myself from humiliation, I walked over to the Acacius and the children.

"Who are you?" the youngest boy asked me. He had such an air of innocence about him that would serve him well.

"I'm Anthony. Who are you?"

"Orion. My parents are dead. You, all of you hate us, you fear us." His voice was strained and pain came from him. The mind and body of a child, confused, vulnerable and scared and surrounded by beings that did indeed see his very existence as a threat. I wasn't about to lie to him. In the future he would trust me more for being honest.

"Not hate," I argued "We're afraid of what you could become. There's a balance, an order to each existence in this world and every time," and I emphasised this after all I'd gone through. "Every single time some creature or other tries to upset that, all Hell breaks loose, and let me tell you, even as an immortal, fear and chaos follow. We—including yourselves—nearly died tonight when this happened. But death is too light a word, to be trapped for all time in a realm of demons, of screeching wraiths without escape, immortality of torment and pain. That is why we fear your existence. Do you understand?"

I know it was a lot, like the Grimm Fairy Tales used to scare children into not walking off with strangers, but these children *were* like the monsters of Grimm. Teach them now or pay later.

"I think so," the boy said. "My father despised me, though he didn't say it. Our parents feared us." Turning to Damien and Nicolas, he said, "But you don't? Damien, you're similar to us? You're part demon, I smell it, just like her." He pointed to Rachel.

Kids, how I love when they point out everyone's secrets. So Damien was part demon.

"No, I'm not afraid of you, but I've seen more than most," Nicolas added. "And I don't fear death. I see your potential, a dream realised. What are your names?"

"Gabriel. And that's Michael and Orion. We already know we are powerful, we felt that fear in our parents."

My curiosity filled for the time being, I wandered over to Marcus. He sighed, then grinned at me and as we walked away, put his arm around my shoulder, like an older, wiser brother. He was so much larger than me I was dwarfed by his size. It was good to hear his voice again, reverberating and low like some mythical creature from a tale.

"I'm sorry about you and her, I truly am. After all you went through, but look now we're both free to do as we please, let's go hunt? And not with the app, the old-fashioned way." He winked.

My spirits lifted having him there. God knows the relief, the happiness that my friend was alive. But a chasm of emptiness still sat in my core and I couldn't bear to look at Rachel staring so intently as Damien. So I left with Marcus.

My eyes were starting to close as drowsiness hit me and I realised I was really hungry. My body ached badly from being thrown around by that creature, that giant of a demon in the fight, and the subsequent battle.

"We thought you were damned," I said.

"Well, nothing happened that I'm aware of. As I said, everything went black and cold and then nothing until I woke up with Emidius and Jamie standing over me. You want to know what they told me, right."

"Of course!"

"As she said, after the Elite were shattered, there was, *or is* no authority in the vampire world. Well, at least not here. Their authority actually covered most of the UK."

"And I'm truly grateful that she saved you, but why you? I mean I would've thought she'd want a vampire to run vampires? It makes no sense. Will other vampires follow a nephilim?"

"Well, it makes perfect sense. I am seen at least as having more control over my emotions, over decisions than most vampires, and I and others will ensure some sort of order is maintained in the supernatural world. It was timing as well. She is going to talk with Sabian, Acacius and get us to form a council. A council of supernatural beings, which has never been done before. It's exciting, and judging by the fallout of what happened, with the children, I'd say just in time. Who knows, maybe in the future one of those children may sit on the council."

"*A council of supernatural beings.* That *is* pretty cool. I don't have to join I hope, I've never been one for rules." I laughed

"No, Anthony, you don't."

We kept our hunting brief that night, too tired for much exertion, on my part anyway. Marcus stayed at my flat, not wanting to go back to his as the last time he was there, he died. We had to divert there to grab some of his clothes. I could hardly lend him mine, with our size difference, and he waited outside whilst I went to grab clothes and various personal belongings he wanted.

Walking back through the city towards my flat, dawn was nearing and I could hear the first rustle of birds waking. A few people went about their business or were returning after a night's drinking and it was surreal and refreshing to see, to feel the normality of it all. No wraiths screaming from humans, no demons. Just humans and animals and crisp morning air.

My flat was peaceful, no odd feelings of being watched and I felt revived enough after the blood to have a quick shower.

"Can I have a shower first? I know you were fighting the good fight and all, but I was *dead*! I smell of death, that isn't good," Marcus joked.

"*That* is going to be your excuse for everything now, isn't it?" I laughed. "Sure, I've to hand it to you, it *is* a good excuse!"

I threw clean sheets on my bed whilst he washed. I couldn't wait to sleep, and it was comforting to have a friend there after all I'd been through.

After my wash, we sat on the bed for a while in our joggers and T-shirts and mused over the last few months.

"I have lived so much since I met you, Anthony. Time loops, shadow people, lycans, blood. And now this future, this council of supernaturals," Marcus added excitedly. He sat cross-legged on the bed, and I did the same.

Reflecting back, I answered, "Well, you did want to find Emidius for so long. She's an interesting being. She's not human. I think the term demi-god is to pacify our interest. I'm not sure she's human at all." He nodded in agreement before continuing,

"She *was* human- a long time ago. But that being said, yeah, it's funny how life turns out. I wanted her to help me for so long, I gave up hope, and then boom! I met you, though you have to admit you thought at first my motives were, well, not just."

I interrupted him, "You can't blame me- that was your fault! When we first met, that look you gave Rachel- and to look at you! You look like a movie star, I don't!" I laughed. "But you were trusting, and honest," I added.

He smiled, "I was out of my depth," and nodding, "I do remember how she looked to me, but you did also. Two vampires walking hand in hand. I sensed something different from you both, maybe it was just because you were holding hands walking- I had never seen vampires do that before. And I thought, I want that! I want that closeness with another. I'm sorry, I shouldn't have brought that up," he looked down as he spoke and groaned.

It didn't matter now, that was over, doomed. I said, "But apparently, you weren't damned for drinking blood. That makes you wonder."

He nodded. Even though he was nephilim, and even though a blinding divine light—apparently the Seraphim—had succeeded in wiping out the demons and wraiths, I still didn't prescribe to his Old Testament beliefs.

He continued, laughing, "And don't think I fancy you because I'm sharing your bed. I just can't go back to my flat again."

"No worries, of course you can't. That would be macabre. It's like the old times when you first stayed with me."

"C'mon, let's sleep. I'm bushed."

Sleep came fast and deep for both of us. We slept for two days solid.

When we woke, we went to see Acacius and find out what was happening with these kids. I also wanted to catch up with Nathaniel, and I guessed he had returned quickly to his hedonistic lifestyle. He may be good and bad, very bad really, but he was a part of me and I wanted, craved companionship of immortals like myself.

Walking through the city, obviously I have no fear of humans, but you can feel alienated when everyone around you is so weak and so mortal. So fragile...

After we had walked about a mile, he spoke first. "They killed their mothers, drank their blood to survive." He shivered at the thought.

"I thought the purebred nephilim killed the parents!" I shrieked.

Marcus replied, "I guess instinct drove them to it. I hope. God knows. What a situation."

I really wanted to ask him about Damien, but I knew I shouldn't, not now at least. Rachel and I had split up due to my irrational emotions and stupid inconsistent behaviour, but I never stopped loving her. Marcus knew about him. Being able to read minds was every nephilim's forte. And to prove it he spoke in a matter of fact tone, "Give it time, Anthony. Don't worry about that now. I'm not going to speak of Damien, but he isn't all he appears. Don't worry, he's not dangerous. He just not quite what he seems."

"Thanks, now I'm more interested and worried!"

"Don't be. Rachel fought and killed a demon, and Lucius was powerful. She's stronger now and probably hasn't found herself yet. When you, as you know, go through an immense change, you need time to adjust. And usually when you've done that you go back to the ones you know, like us. Our friendship is a comfort."

"I see. Good to know."

My phone buzzed in my coat. It was Nicolas, I didn't even know how he'd got my number, but I knew before I answered it trouble had arrived.

His voice was frantic. "Orion has escaped us! He sneaked out of his room and we have no idea where he is. One of us has to stay here, that'll be me, to watch over the others. Can you help?"

"You know I will. Where did he live? He may have gone back home."

"In the centre somewhere. Hang on." I could hear Nicolas talking to Damien.

"It's Nicolas. Orion has gone. They want me to find him," I told Marcus though he no doubt knew being telepathic.

"Anthony, we think it was around Abbey Green. You'll help?"

"Of course. I'll keep you posted. Where are the others? Out searching?"

"They've just left now!"

"Nicolas," I spoke quickly.

"Yes?"

"Don't lose any more..." I hung up.

"He's probably gone to his home just off the centre of the city."

"Abbey Green? I heard. Come on, let's find him. He's probably scared."

"To be honest it's not him I'm worried about!" So, turning on our heels, we headed back into the city.

Abbey Green is hidden away in a quiet, cobbled square with a huge sycamore tree in the centre which reigns down over like a huge natural umbrella. This is one of the oldest parts of the city and you often find supernatural creatures living in the oldest places, clinging onto their past as some semblance of security throughout the centuries. No doubt his mother had lived nearby until the boy had, through his instincts, bled her dry. A macabre start in life for them all, draining their mothers and something which I didn't want to think about.

"I can feel he's been close by," Marcus whispered and stopped abruptly.

"Orion," I called softly. "Orion, its Anthony. Are you alright?"

Marcus raised his eyebrows, questioning my calling the child, but there was no point in trying to sneak up on him. He no doubt knew we were here before we sensed him.

We heard his laughter and followed it to a little street alongside the square, and there he was, talking to a group of vampires dressed in Victorian finery and wearing masks. Something about them made me feel queasy, and the way they were laughing and petting him, and his innocent sounding giggling seemed to astonish and delight them. They were clearly fascinated with him. We stepped up a pace. "Orion! We were worried. Are you alright?"

He turned to look at us, his cherub mouth dropped, and he took a step back, closer to the group of decadent strangers.

"*You* are not his parents!" one of them stated, looking at us sternly. He was taller than the others and wearing a top hat and tails, immaculately dressed, but the masks seemed as odd as the clothing. Their whole demeanour had changed. They'd been laughing, smiling and now their faces resembled stone, hard and rigid.

"Who are you?" Marcus asked puzzled. They were not only dressed in antique clothing, something about them, they seemed from a bygone era.

"No friend of yours!" A woman dressed in black silk and lace, so delicate that her bustle dress shifted as she moved, shimmering under the antiquated street lights.

A roar of thunder bellowed fast and pitch blackness fell and seconds later the light came back. And they were gone, with Orion.

My eyes flickered as I adjusted to the shock wave, and at first neither of us spoke.

"I cannot sense him." Marcus's first words full of panic. "What's that noise?"

A buzzing sound, like a huge wasp persisted around us. Tilting our heads back, we saw a flock of drones hoovering over and around us.

"What the fuck is that? Where did all those come from? Why are they bothering us?" But I had no time to continue as red lasers flashed onto us and instinctively we both fled, back into the square and though a tunnelled walkway alongside a shop. We didn't speak with words but expressions, our eyes, and mouths wide with horror and confusion.

It made no difference; the drones simply tracked us, and were now firing at us. Without needing to say anything else, we flew out of there as fast as our preternatural legs would go. At the exit, Marcus grabbed me, his huge wings opening up and swooped us so high and so fast that I instinctively closed my eyes. My head was spinning. Luckily, we didn't fly into any other immortals. After about ten minutes, we lost them and found ourselves on the outskirts of the city and rushed to get into Rachel's home. But it was different.

The beautiful old front door had been replaced with some kind of metallic atrocity and the whole street contained high security and cameras. It was like something from a nightmare.

Without words, we turned on our heels and fled, not wanting to attract the drones, and headed further off out of the city until we came to a derelict building. Though it was not entirely abandoned as I sensed others around, a scattering of both mortals and immortals were hidden there-about.

"What the shit just happened?" Marcus spluttered. Even for us, we were both out of breath.

"I have no clue. What the Hell was all that?" I sat down on the floor to cool down and get my breath back.

"Where did those drones come from, and Rachel's *house*!"

"As much as it makes me feel sick saying this, and even saying it makes me feel like I'm jinxing something, have we fallen into another time loop? Is that what that roar of thunder and blackness was? At least we both have experience and should be able to get our way home, as long as we don't end up dead first!"

"I don't know, Anthony; this is nothing like the time loop we were in! This is *our* world with *drones*. And the houses—that security, bars on windows. Something's definitely screwed up here. We need to find the others. We'll have to edge around the city, stick to the tree lines and plan it out. Why were they firing at us? And who the fuck are *they*?"

The building we took shelter in was an old Victorian industrial structure. It hadn't been used for decades and I was keen to speak with the others hidden thereabouts to find out what was happening. It was nearly midnight and I had recovered after that bizarre and terrifying incident, although I was acutely aware that I was hungry. As we crept around, we both jumped suddenly when we heard sirens going off around the city. What now? It was like being in a dystopian parallel reality.

Marcus looked at me. I saw blue lights flashing outside, but to my relief they kept on going past the window. I sensed tension in that place from others hiding there and through the thick dust and rubble of the decay, I went in search of answers.

I didn't have to look far as the other immortals there were seeking us out. They looked ragged, not like the foul beasts that turned me, but from their clothing and appearance it was obvious that they lived rough permanently.

"Who are you?" a voice barked at me.

I could see a vampire partially hidden in the shadows. I had so many questions, but better to answer his first. Marcus answered, "I'm Marcus, and this is Anthony. You're vampires, like us?"

The vampire looked apprehensive and his group of four stood with their backs to the entrance of the room as if ready to flee at any second. Grime so thick it looked like a coating of brown skin mixed with rust red on the archaic machinery that lay to waste, and a fierce wind blew through the vandalised windows.

Trying to muster his authority and courage, the young male vampire stepped forward a little into the light, "Where are you from? You're not like us. We haven't seen you before. Why is that?"

"We haven't been here before," I answered honestly.

"Are they hunting you? If you've been seen, they won't stop until they've captured you."

"No, we just arrived here. We're looking for some old friends. Nathaniel, Damien, and Nicolas. Do you know of them? Two of them at least are vampires. Damien is a hybrid."

At that last word, the young vampire's eyes narrowed and his jaw clenched. He looked at me with hostility. "You're looking for a hybrid? Are you fucking mad? You are friends with *them*?"

I knew there was something wrong here—terribly wrong. There is bigotry in the supernatural world, but generally not this fierce.

"Damien is half vampire, half demon," Marcus answered calmly.

The vampire nodded and looked somewhat calmer. "I see, I thought you meant...the blood angels. Where have you come from and how do you both look so clean? How do you *exist*?"

By this point I could detect no threat from him, I looked to Marcus who nodded slightly in agreement. We would need help in this Hellhole and that meant trusting someone. We had to start somewhere.

"Before we tell you, can we go somewhere else? It doesn't feel safe here, even for a vampire." But as I finished speaking, I heard a screech so loud we had to cover our ears. He didn't speak, just signalled his head in the direction of the door to follow him.

They led us to a damp basement and two of them pushed shut a heavy wooden door, and we all waited in silence for ages.

Whispering he spoke, "That was close." A tiny candle barely lit up the room, which like upstairs was full of ancient looking machinery and rubbish. And dust. But it smelt worse than it looked. I couldn't discern much more of its surroundings, and then I told them what had happened.

"We were following a child in the city, and found him speaking to some vampires, they were dressed in Victorian costume and wearing masks. Then a flash of lightening, a roar of thunder and the next they had vanished and were chased by drones! Drones, where did they come from?"

He frowned, looked at the others who shrugged, then asked me, "What do you mean? Where do you come from? We've had drones for nearly a decade now? I don't understand you?"

Marcus interjected, "This must be a time loop or something, we *live* in Bath. But it seems not in the same time...or something." He joined this vampire in frowning too.

"A time loop? No, this isn't a time loop, this is the twenty-first century, pure and simple." Closing his eyes for a second, the vampire continued, "There was a tale, more of a legend, that said the first of them was stolen from time and taken back to the year of eighteen-hundred and something."

"Who, who was taken?" I asked. As soon as the words left my mouth I could feel Marcus's stare boring into me. "Orion? Those masked vampires? No, that's inconceivable. I've heard some stuff, seen more than I've wanted but no..." I shook my head in disbelief.

Marcus wasn't always known for his patience. Or his sense. Rather than continue with the story of the fact that *we* may have witnessed the incident that caused this shift, he asked, "These blood angels, have you ever seen one?"

"Most of us haven't. Few have and lived to tell. They're ruthless. They like nothing more than to feed on other immortals, our blood being more potent. They don't look like us, they're bigger. Their hands are like claws, their wings and skin are dark and touched red from all the blood they gorge on. No one, not even us, goes out after the alarms. And like you, they have wings, we do not."

"That was a curfew?"

"How the hell don't you know this? Who are you?"

My mind was spinning with all this new information and this horrible situation. *Bloody hell Acacius and Damien,* they had one thing to do.

My words tumbled out fast. "I think we've come from another time or dimension. We know of these blood angels, but where we are from they're only children and there are only three. In our world, there are no drones that shoot at you, no curfew, and our kind, we live well."

"I want to visit your world." The vampire's face lit up as if we could offer him paradise.

"How do you hunt, if you are hunted?" I asked.

"Not easily. Most of us have survived on the outskirts of cities, going out before the curfew and we have to hunt in packs. We used technology at first. That worked and it was safe, but those bastards, both government and blood angels, managed to decipher that and track us. So now we have to hunt as our ancestors, except they weren't hunted by something far worse."

"So how do the mortals cope?"

"They have personal drones, in and outside their homes. Drones fitted with guns, tranquilizers. Cameras monitor everywhere. Everything is on lock down at eleven anyway, unless you have a permit. That requires either signing one at your own risk, but they don't usually allow that because the blood angels might turn you into one of their own. They increased their numbers before the curfews came. Or you need extra security, and even if you buy it, it has to be from those crazy or desperate enough to provide you with it."

"Oh God!" I sat back in the filth to try to comprehend the disaster. Marcus was quicker...

"Orion! Those masked vampires snatched him... That must have been why they were dressed like that. They were from an earlier century! A time loop. I think we know how this happened."

As I heard the words and pieced it together, tension gripped my body. "And that place, I was only thinking earlier on how it is the oldest section of the city, and how many paranormals dwell there," I groaned.

We looked at each other, and I spoke. "If we could get back to that place—it may have to be the same time, hell the same date—in theory we could skip into that loop and stop all this. Are we on drugs or something?" I had to laugh, to release the fear and the intensity of our situation.

"God, I wish we were. Drugs would be easy compared. That is the best plan we have. What was the date it happened? 30th April 2016? What is it now?

The other vampire spoke. "18th February; thereabouts."

"What year?"

"2016, so you've only time travelled back two months then!" he sniggered.

"Two months. I don't want to wait for two months living like this. Can you help us find our friends and tell us of, of *this* place?"

"What is this old building?" He grinned. I couldn't blame him, it was incredible but I wasn't about to live in the gutter, hunted by man and immortals.

"Nathaniel, nope never heard of him. Nor Nicolas. There are very few of us here. We'll help you, if you help us.

"What's your name?"

"My name is Kyle; this is Nikki, Anne, and Trish. We live like rats. Once, I'm told, we lived like kings.

"Kyle, I can't promise you'll live like a king, but if you help us, you will be, by default, helping yourselves. We have to try and find our friends, but maybe they're not here... God, I hate these time loop things."

Marcus took me aside. "It's confusing, but if they've taken Orion back in time, these blood angels are no doubt his descendants. We probably won't find the others. They may not even exist in this reality. But that place where we saw the masked vampires, that must be where the time loop or whatever it is, is? I think first we need to know more about this time; we can't navigate through a terrain we don't know."

That was the best start. And trusting Kyle and his friends was a good choice; they knew their time and could show us.

"We'd like to be included in your conversations, if we're to help each other!" Kyle added.

"We know where in the city Orion was taken, and we know who by, although we know nothing about them. He was snatched by masked vampires dressed in ninetieth century clothing- just like your legends told. Once they grabbed him, a crash of thunder blasted and everything went pitch black. Then we arrived here. That must be a time loop, of sorts."

Kyle spoke slowly, his eyes darting around the room, "So, you're saying, I think, that you two come from a parallel reality? In your reality, Orion, and the others like him are children. In our time", he gestured to his friends, "Our time now, this is the result of those masked vampires stealing Orion and taking him back in time. Because of that, because of what they have done, he has bred and we have this plague of his kind in *our* reality?"

"Exactly that!" Marcus replied and sighed loudly.

Trish spoke next. She, like all of them looked ready to fight, their clothing, urban combat. Jeans, custom made armour and boots with an array of weapons strapped to their hips and legs. She was tall and curvaceous; her dark hair fell down her shoulders, but this wasn't a fashion statement. She was a survivor, a warrior. "If you find the time loop entrance, and you get in, you'll have to find Orion. Then you'll have to bring him back, somehow. But how will you know where you'll end up? You could go anywhere. And even if you get to the nineteenth century, you'll still have to find him. And, I'm not being rude, but neither of you look like you belong in that century."

The others looked at each other uneasily. Nikki spoke to us all. Contrary to Trish, her hair was purest white. They all looked like vampire warriors from the future, which I guess they were, an alternative dystopian future that I had no desire to stay in.

"I know what you're thinking, they'll need help. As I see it, they need the help of a necromancer, and there's not many of them left." Nikki paused here, her eyes scrunched as she thought. "We do know of a few, but they are dangerous and erratic."

"You're world *is* dangerous and erratic, I don't see what choice we have," I said softly. I was less concerned than them about these blood angels. Heck, I'd drink them before they could kill me. Maybe that would get me killed, but I'd rather that than die on my knees.

"But first, tell us of your world, tell us everything," I asked. "How long has it been like this? The drones, the blood angels, the curfews?"

Their daggers caught the gleam of that meagre candlelight in the basement of the building. Kyle was a towering figure, but he had gentleness about him. None of them had a mean streak; they were tired of this exhausting existence.

One of the female vampires spoke in answer to my question. "It has always been like this for us. I was made vampire, like Kyle and Trish and Nikki sometime in the last two decades. Those of us with family that are still alive, very occasionally we look on them but we cannot seek them out fully. There is too much danger for them and us. What else do you want to know?"

I nodded as I took in her information. "In my life I live well as a vampire, I have sources of income and a place to live, as does Marcus. We even have an app to trace evil doers, we collect their digital information and those of their acquaintance. Under normal circumstances, though to be honest I haven't had many of those, we have no threats."

They looked astonished. "We don't have money in this age. There is no need, everyone does what their talent, or passion draws to them to. Everything is on a credit system—food, housing, entertainment. Everyone is registered," Anne continued.

"As we are not on the radar so to speak, not being human, we have to live out here. Everything is controlled, every person accounted for. The humans live well. About thirty years ago, society changed. Living was too perilous. Blood angels were growing in number, most die at their hands, some are changed. The governments made a decision; humans would strive to be better, to do what their talents possessed, and not to labour for money or materialism. Living so close to death daily inspired a new world order. But with that came control. Money is only available through criminal means, bartering is the only real form of currency now."

Marcus and I were silent for some time. It was an apocalyptic nightmare. As Anne had said, living in such close proximity of death had made the authorities re-examine human existence but it also gave people less control.

Marcus asked, "The drones? So many..."

"They are mainly for human protection. blood angels do on occasion go into the city. They used to go in day or night. Policing that with people is too heavy on manpower so they developed drones with the capability of firing. They obviously monitor the mortals, but I do believe in the main it's for their protection," Anne answered. "Either way, you cannot sustain a population that turns entirely into vampires—hybrid or otherwise."

As she finished, as if on cue we heard the screeching again far off in the distance of one of those creatures. It sent shivers down my spine and a hush fell over us.

"They are a hybrid of our species, can't they be reasoned with?"

Nikki resumed the tale, "It's said that in the beginning they were reasonable and lived alongside other supernaturals. But over time they chose to breed. We don't know *how* that's possible, but they did so between themselves to keep their blood line pure. In short, they're interbred, much like the aristocracy of the past. And like the aristocracy, madness reigns. They cannot be reasoned with now, because they *have* no reason."

"And Orion?" Marcus murmured. "Does anyone ever speak his name? If he's alive, we may be able to reason with him?"

"We know the name, the tales. We know he originated here in this city after a battle of demons. We know nothing else. Understand every night for us is a battle of existence. It's already late now," Kyle added hastily.

"We have to hunt, so we'll take you with us. We only talk when we need to. When we're out, everything is monitored. The old ways still hold, we try and only take the evil, and after curfew, it is mostly only the malevolent mortals that are out there. This tiny city has a strong population of blood angels. If what you've told us is true, that would be the reason why. We stay out of the city, especially tonight," Anne whispered.

"But you said you hunt before the curfew, is that because of us arriving here?"

Kyle nodded and they readied themselves to leave.

Marcus and I were stunned with the revelations of where we had ended up but we'd been through enough crazy already and so prepared ourselves for what the night would bring. A more sinister part of my nature revealed that I wanted to see these blood angels for myself, and even try to reason with them. I wasn't afraid of them and I could sense that neither was Marcus. But more importantly, once we had the lay of the land so to speak, we would need to find a necromancer or the like and get through that time loop. And that in itself raised a thousand questions.

But for now, we headed off towards the city and I saw that Kyle, Trish, and the others, like us headed for the many parks that small city has. There were less drones this far out, the odd one here and there and we heard it long before seeing it and by then we had all taken shelter. Whispering I asked them, "Why hasn't any of our kind created something to block the drone's detection, or signal? I know this can be done; something to do with frequencies?"

"You're right, and some years ago some were able to do this, but they adapted them and update them constantly. Our predicament prevents us. Had we more money maybe we could try?"

They definitely needed to improve their situation, but I thought it best not to state the obvious. I was new here, so I may have not fared better if I were them. But this was a miserable existence.

We came across a gang of men doing some kind of shady business deep within the park, and slowly we crept forth, circling out to surround them. In the distance, I could hear that infernal buzzing of drones and I knew then that if I had to stay here I would make it my life's mission to get rid of those things.

As we approached and stayed hidden in the parks tree line again I heard that screeching sound. "Why do they do that? Surely, they don't want to announce their presence. That's just dumb!"

"They don't think like us. They're removed and see themselves as top of the food chain. Governments cannot contain or control them; their will, their survival, predatory instincts are above anything. Usually they wail when they have caught someone, a wail of victory."

I wasn't impressed and my stomach churned at that thought. They sounded primitive, but by announcing where they were, that could help Marcus and me. He looked at me and a slight grin upturned his lips as if he had the same thought.

"Their confidence in themselves, having none to challenge them helps us, gives us the advantage," he offered.

Peering out through the trees, I heard the faintest sound and looked up to see a shape. Like giant bat type wings circling and then it shot off. A lump came to my throat, and I remembered the size of the children- how their features had seemed too big for their stature. I guess they're all grown up now.

There were four criminals, nothing unusual about them, but Nikki raised a hand for us to stop. Here in this time, these vampires would determine what crime was going on, in case they could gain from it. The crime, not unusual, was drugs and a vast amount of money was being handed over. We pounced and within minutes, we were satiated and they were dead.

We picked up the money and searched their belongings. Their phones were different from what I was used to.

"Leave the phones!" Trish whispered urgently. "Every phone, including these, have tracking devices. It's too risky to use."

I couldn't believe it! I would have no phone. That is living in the dark ages.

Marcus muttered to me, "I don't want to wait in the dust here anymore."

Before we could do anything, Anne whipped out a scalpel and took hold of one the criminal's right hand, making a clean incision between the thumb and finger. Trish was alongside and holding up a small transparent plastic bag. With tweezers, Anne produced a tiny chip and popped this in the bag. They did the same with all the others.

"We'll have to dispose of the bodies, otherwise these are useless. We have a place to do this."

We hadn't realised just how organised these dystopian vampires were, and we hadn't noticed that Nikki had slipped away and pulled up with a car.

"It was theirs," she said indicating to the criminals. "I found it by their scent. C'mon, let's get the bodies in."

We couldn't go with them, as there wasn't room, but decided we would go back to their hide out. We would need a chip if we wanted to get around without those drones shooting us.

"Will the drones sense we're not human?"

"Fortunately, they're not that sophisticated yet. Kyle is our tech expert. He'll take these to friends, they'll alter them, and then you can use them," Anne explained.

"What's the price?" I asked.

"Freedom of course. Take us with you. If you don't, we won't help you, and you won't get anywhere fast without these. Remember, humans *know* of our existence, that's why every single human has personal security and why every single human is chipped. It's done at birth. The drones can detect you fast. But with these..." Kyle held the plastic bag of ID chips from Trish. "With these, you'll have an easier time, you'll be accounted for."

"So, these chips don't hold facial recognition tech?" I asked.

"Wear a hood and don't look up much. In the main they just register your details, address, function, age and there's no alarm unless you have a criminal record. Or, unless you don't register at all- but you know that from earlier!"

"But they were criminals. I'm sorry to fire fifty questions at you!" I asked.

"Criminals usually have the cleanest tags. We all have ex criminal tags in us. You still need to use the precautions and avoid the city centre especially after curfew. But you'll get by with them."

All I could think about was getting back to my own time, where we didn't have surveillance on this epic scale and masses of the crazed beasts flying around.

We met back at their hide out, minus Kyle and Nikki who were busy burying the dead and altering the new tags.

They seemed calmer now and the night was still. No sirens, no wails from the winged demons, just silence.

"How did you all come to know each other?

Trish answered, "We came to find each other quite easily, you know yourself it's a small city, and to survive we have to stick together. We have other friends, contacts but it's best to stick in small groups to avoid detection."

"Do you always kill your prey?" I tried not to sound judgemental or shocked. I couldn't judge them anyhow after the amount I had killed, that was something I was fairly good at blocking from my mind most of the time. Tonight brought it home, now I was able to control my emotions. A long time coming, that.

"Not at all. But we wanted their chips, and without their chips—even had we managed to extract these from them whilst keeping them alive—they would be detected, and in that, so would we. As it goes, you needed these ID's. So long as you're not actually picked up by the authorities, you'll be alright and no one in the authorities will be wiser. As for the criminals, their families, friends, they'll be too scared to report it, seeing as though they're felons. They'll assume the blood angels have them, and that would pose an investigation into their families, their friends and so on."

Marcus asked, "So we can't go into the city without the chips?"

"What happened to you last time? In the city, drones monitor everyone; they scan for ID chips. If you don't have one, they assume you're a criminal, since you aren't registered. The penalty is death, or worse, prison. If your ID matches their database, you're clear. If not, well...you know that already." She paused here. "Before this, the blood angels would roam the streets. They managed somehow to blend in, at least in the darker hours. They left carnage. Everything went bat-shit crazy. Military were deployed but even they couldn't cope with the amount of deaths. Tagging became compulsory."

"What a messed-up world, all because of *one* hybrid! We'll still need to access the time loop. You spoke of a necromancer, or someone who can help us enter it. We have experience of time portals, but this is different. I want to see if those strange vampires still appear, or if we need something to help get us through it!" Marcus sounded as determined as me to get out of here and get the boy back.

"There are some that might be able to help. We can ask. Our world is a tight community so someone is bound to know someone. Necromancers tend to hate our kind and on paper, they look like model citizens, but I suspect there'll be some who will find this too interesting to resist. Night is nearly over, we would be better off going tomorrow at early evening."

Kyle and Trish came back with our tags and a needle to inject them in our hands. It wasn't particularly painful, but I was keen to see just what information these held before injecting it.

They produced a hand-held device and held this over the chip. There were names, dates of birth, addresses, and occupations. Under *Legal Information* there was nothing—meaning we had no criminal record—and a general health status. It was creepy, but it had to done. I'd get it out afterwards, and I ensured they didn't put it too deep in our hands.

And so, we were ready. We chatted to them about their civilisation. How people no longer worked in jobs to pay bills. Obviously, there were people who were happy with less demanding work and found their pleasure in other ways, but society was encouraged to find a meaningful outlet for work. How far you progressed and what contributions you made determined your status. Wealth was no longer the driving force and living to work, to pay bills, and accumulating stuff was an archaic system. It seemed that as death was so close in everyday life, living took on a new meaning and was celebrated more. But we would still change it, if we could.

As Kyle and the others settled down to rest after the night's hunting, I took Marcus aside. I needed to speak to him in private. We wandered up out of the basement and found a small, dusty room at the back of the building.

Pulling the amulet out of my pocket, I said, "Maybe Jamie can help? He said he's been to other realities with Emidius. It has to be worth trying. But I need some privacy."

"Sure, I'll watch out for you. You think maybe he can get us back? I hope so; this time is crazy!"

As Marcus stood on look out, I held the strange amulet in my hands, grasping it and concentrating on Jamie, as he had told me to do. I had to feel him here, feel his presence in the room. Seeing his gregarious smile in my mind, happiness swelled throughout me. My mouth curve up instinctively. He was a good friend. For a split second, I saw him before me and opened my eyes but then he was gone. Hollowness replaced warmth and happiness. I knew then I could not reach him, at least not yet. I refused to believe that time stood in our way since time is a human concept and Jamie now travelled beyond human conceptions.

Marcus turned around from the doorway, "I felt warmth for a moment."

"I'll try again, but not right now. We need to get that time loop anyway." Putting it back in my pocket, we went down to the basement to join the others who were sleeping amongst the dust.

Book 3 Release End of Feb 18. Sign up to keep informed, receive goodies or join my ARC team or all of the above! Get a taster below...

Always Dark Angel Subscribe[1]
alwaysdarkangel.com[2]

Join my Moon Council of the Supernatural[3] Facebook group where I show cover reveals, chat about animals, the paranormal-like what's your favourite paranormal tv show and mythical creatures and generally hang out.

---

1. http://alwaysdarkangel.us11.list-manage.com/sub-scribe?u=91bae505ec825948a210493f9&id=e46c6bc853

2. https://alwaysdarkangel.com/

3. https://www.facebook.com/groups/247165435816384/?ref=bookmarks

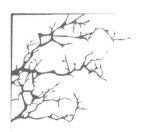

About

JN MOON IS A NEW AUTHOR who has currently written three books in her first Urban Fantasy Series. She writes Paranormal Thrillers/ Urban Fantasy.

She can be found wandering in nature, reading or upside down.

Not that she thinks she's a vampire bat, she enjoys aerial arts.

And likes hanging upside down... She's also an aficionado air guitarist.

She lives with a myriad of animals and loves nothing better than talking to like-minded souls so get in touch. You don't have to like hanging upside down, but it helps...

Email: alwaysdarkangel@hotmail.co.uk

Twitter: alwaysdarkangel[1]

Facebook: Moon Council of the Supernatural[2]

Web: alwaysdarkangel.com[3]

---

1. https://twitter.com/alwaysdarkangel

2. https://www.facebook.com/groups/247165435816384/?ref=bookmarks

3. http://alwaysdarkangel.us11.list-manage.com/sub-
   scribe?u=91bae505ec825948a210493f9&id=e46c6bc853

Author Notes

I GOT THE IDEA OF A dark nephilim whilst listening to a particular song, and then spent weeks researching the nephilim in old texts online. I did a lot of thinking on my commute, I knew his name would be Marcus and he would have slate grey eyes. When I researched nephilim, they were recorded to have grey eyes. Not that really existed, but it's fun to imagine. I've always loved mythology and as a kid was entranced by films like Sinbad and Jason and the Argonauts.

A celestial creature, the nephilim falls from grace. After centuries of fighting evil he succumbs to temptation and wonder...for Marcus the consequences are dire but we've all done that, though not literally! With my research obviously nephilim were not recorded as drinking vampire blood, it was said that if an under-worlder tried to drink the blood of a fallen angel this was the most heinous crime, so turning this around, I was excited to explore this as a story.

I loved the creation of him and his contrasting character with Anthony. With references of the thinning of the veil, these came from the history of Halloween or Samhain as pagans call it. The time where the spirit world is closest to the living, and the consequences of Marcus's actions, wraiths of hate in man's heart pour out along with demons to destroy all. And also that flawed, darker characters could make a difference.

Acacius, in contrast to most of the characters seems a pure character driven to a just cause but his past reveals pain and actually he is driven more by the desire to avoid that pain.

Demons; I researched them. Demonology isn't as scary or grand as it sounds. Mostly I found they spend their time having sex with humans, I kind of thought, is that it? Surely anything done to excess would become boring after a century or less. So with Lucius I added that extra, he was malevolent but he was also well read in magic and he had a cause, though it cost him.

I did a ton of research, I do for all my characters. Nephilim were interesting to research, some bits that were edited out as they didn't move the story forward, but revealed how Acacius and his company wiped out the experimentals from book 1. I'll either put that in another story or send out these writings to you, readers. They're a story in themselves, and I visited Wells cathedral to get pictures, feelings of where that battle would take place.

I write what I want to read and what I think you the reader will find refreshing and a little different. I pour everything into my writing. I'm grateful to have you here, reading. This was once a dream and I've had a steep learning curve and I'm always studying the craft and reading whilst doing the 9-5 thing.

When I've been through hard times, getting into bed at the end of the day with a book has often been my saving grace. To lose yourself in another world.

I have a lot of pictures on pinterest that I take inspiration from when I'm writing my character biography's. There's a link below if you want to look.

Contact me if you have any thoughts, what did you like, what would you like to have read here. Writing is a two way process, and how I see/ feel about my book will be totally different from you. That in itself is fascinating.

Thanks for reading this and allowing me to fill your imagination.

pinterest.co.uk/taoistjo/ Note: there are possible spoilers/ teasers for upcoming book ideas here.

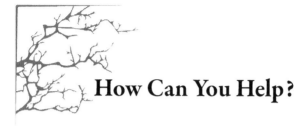

How Can You Help?

THE MOST POTENT THING a writer can have is reviews. Without support from happy, loyal fans we fade into nothing not having the clout of the celebrity writers.

If you enjoyed this please leave a review. Some stars, a few words are all it takes. **Just three minutes of your time.**

JN Moon USA[1]
JN Moon UK[2]
Thank You,
JO

---

1. https://www.amazon.com/JN-MOON/e/B00DTUJIRE/

2. https://www.amazon.co.uk/JN-MOON/e/B00DTUJIRE/

Printed in Great Britain
by Amazon